Casualties of Peace

Gene editing toward a new world order

A novel

by

Harold H. Lee

ISBN-13: 978-1544754642
ISBN-10: 1544754647

First Edition

To my dear wife

Soong Wei

宋

薇

who has left the planet Earth.

Acknowledgement

I am grateful for the encouragement of Paz Layug Reyes and Robert Ruben in the course of working on the manuscript. I would also like to thank Mac McPherson, Dr. Jerry Williams, and Dr. Jack Rary for their reading, critique, and helpful suggestions.

The book cover was designed by my twin granddaughters Elizabeth and Esther Morrison aged twelve; I am especially pleased and thank them for their involvement.

I am particularly grateful for the assistance of Peggy P Edwards and Miranda McPhee of the Village Publishing Club (Laguna Woods, CA), without them this work would not have been brought into print.

Harold H. Lee
Mission Viejo, California
2017

"We make war so we may live in peace."

- Aristotle

"Extremism in the defense of liberty [humanity] is no vice.

Moderation in the pursuit of justice [peace] is no virtue."

- Barry Goldwater, 1964

(The words in brackets are those of the author to substitute "liberty" and "justice".)

PROLOGUE

Prior to the 1950s, the formulae for biochemical reactions of metabolisms of living cells could be printed on one page. Then in the seventies, the content of that page increased to fill the surface area of a poster. Stretching your imagination, what is it now? The surface area required is both sides of a 4' x 8' piece of plywood.

Students of molecular biology base their experiments on the dogma: DNA -> RNA -> Protein. That dogma has not changed. The elucidation of the detail of the processes of the dogma has increased just like the biochemical reactions in the metabolic chart.

It has been more than sixty years since the double helix of DNA, deoxyribonucleic acid, was discovered by Watson and Crick. That started the new age of biology. In the intervening years, much progress has been made. With the advent of computer science, discoveries in molecular biology and its applications have been climbing in a logarithmic ascent. The first genetic manipulation by American scientists was to insert human genes into a non-human organism, the bacteria E. coli, to yield a product called Humulin. This product of genetic engineering has become a versatile treatment for diabetes.

At about the same time, Chinese scientists announced they had synthesized a molecule of human insulin in a test tube. The latter work was cumbersome and time-consuming, and therefore not practical for medical application.

With the background of molecular biology, new biomedical treatments have been born for various diseases previously unapproachable with conventional treatments. It is called molecular therapy. In layperson's terms it means treating the roots of the disease rather than the symptoms. For example, Humulin is used to treat diabetes in those unable to make insulin normally. The protein molecules are injected into the patients.

Molecular therapy would correct the defects of the insulin gene in the insulin-producing cells, the beta cells, in the Island of Langerhans in the pancreas.

Gene editing is no longer a theory, it is a demonstrable technology applicable to fight diseases. The versatile major player is the technique called CRISPR-Cas 9—Cluster Regularly-Interspace Short Palindromic Repeats; Cas-9 is the protein nuclease, an enzyme that cleaves DNA.

Nanotechnology will soon become one of the major tools in medical sciences in the treatment of difficult illnesses by the targeted delivery of specific drugs. With monoclonal antibody as the specific guidance system there will be a more accurate delivery and dosage, eliminating much of the waste of the present drug-delivery systems like oral or intravenous routes.

Another future and more versatile creation in not only drug delivery but also communication is the use of robots. Robotic technology at the macro level such as the auto assembly line has already been fully developed. However the development of robotics at micro and nano levels are still in their infancies. Terms like nanobot, biobot, cellbot, tissuebot, etc., will not be strangers to us in the near future. The combination of gene-editing technology and the targeted delivery of specific drugs with nanotechnology will most likely materialize before the middle of this century.

In this novel, I have made use of my limited knowledge of biotechnology and molecular biology to fictionally transform these two disciplines into bioweapons with a peaceful overture in certain geopolitical climates. I have also fictionalized certain facts.

I have taken the liberty of basing many of my fictional characters on friends and relatives because each of them has played an important role of one kind or another, contributing to the richness and wellness of my life. I cannot thank each and every one in more grateful terms than using them in this novel, my first non-professional work. I hope I do them justice in this book.

SHELTER 113, SIBERIA

The wind was still. The sky was pitched dark without a single star. The only sound was the rumble of a cargo train through the desolate Siberian desert in the quietness of the summer night. The only lights were the headlight and two small red lights at the end of the last car of the Trans-Siberian freight train, with a hundred or more cars doing some sixty miles per hour, pulled by twin diesel engines. There had been no rear caboose since the late 1980s. The four engineers could monitor every foot of the mile-long train from the comfort of their driver's seats. A bluish-green glow from the monitors was about all the interior light spilling out from the engine room, other than the soft light emitting from the living quarters just behind the engines.

During this particular starless night, the freight train from Moscow slowed to a stop at a dilapidated station in the middle of the Siberian desert. The last car was detached in front of the station. As soon as the car was unhooked, the train started to move again, gaining speed toward the east coast of Russia. The detached car together with that section of track was slowly lowered some fifty feet into the ground. The car was then rolled off the track into a vast warehouse-like underground structure—it was like a platform in a theater but much larger, large enough to hoist a missile launcher. The track was then raised back up to ground level in just a matter of minutes. Two days later when the train was travelling toward Moscow from the Pacific coast, the reverse procedures would be carried out if necessary.

There was nothing unusual about this particular biweekly freight train between Moscow and the outlet of Russia into the Pacific, the city of Vladivostok. It had no passengers except the engineers who operated the train. On this particular run, they were substitutes for the regular drivers who had been given a special vacation for their work well done without a single mishap in the last six months. For an outsider, this particular run was just another routine trip.

Without very careful and close examination, no one could tell that a particular part of the track in front of the dilapidated station was detachable. In such darkness, with not a soul for miles around, only those who managed the operation knew what was going on. Even in broad daylight this region was the most desolate in the vastness of Siberia. However, with hundreds if not thousands of spy satellites hovering in the sky, one of them might just accidentally detect the changeover. The whole covert operation was always at night. Therefore it was extremely difficult for satellites with spying eyes to detect anything unusual.

GLOBAL FOUNDATION

On a bright sunny autumn afternoon, there was a gathering of close to two hundred rich and generous people in the ballroom of a modest, five-storied brownstone in midtown Manhattan. A simple unornamented sign, Global Foundation, was attached to the front of this 150-year-old Manhattan office building—one of thousands of brownstones on this island of rocks.

On that day, ushers at the front door directed the guests to the spacious ballroom set up with tables. The table settings were modest with good taste—fresh flowers as center pieces with names of persons assigned to that table. These very appropriate settings were done by Jewel's Catering, a catering service that specialized in charity functions that were not too elaborate but not ordinary either.

There was a sort of head table where the officials of the Global Foundation sat. At all the other tables, which each seated eight to ten, were philanthropists from around the world. The seating arrangement for these generous people was random. All the contributors were treated equally regardless of the size of their donations, unlike many charity organizations that would distinguish among big and small donors.

Sitting in the middle of the "head table" at the front was a portly gentleman with a perpetual smile on his face. He was the president of the Global Foundation, Mr. Eric E. Erikson, or Mr. Triple E as known by his coworkers. He was in his mid-fifties. He never talked about the origin of his middle initial E. On his right was Ms. Paz Layug, VP-Operations, who was in her mid-forties. Ms. Layug had a soft and serene-looking face, a face in which someone in distress could find comfort just by looking at her. On Mr. Triple E's left was a tall, redheaded Irishman, Mr. Ian Kennedy, VP-Management. He was also in his mid-forties. Other board members sat at other tables with various philanthropists.

There was an important and practical purpose for such a table arrangement. It was an excellent way for the philanthropists to get to know each other. Although many may be competitors in their business endeavors, they shared a common denominator as donors of the Global Foundation. In the world of business, today's enemy could be tomorrow's partner. This kind of interaction could only benefit the Global Foundation.

The Global Foundation's charity work was unique in character. At the site of any disaster, big or small, members were always the first at the scene before even the Red Cross or other NGOs (non-governmental organizations). They set up tents or tables near the scene of the disaster. Since many were forced to evacuate urgently, they might have nothing but the clothes on their backs; emergency money was handed to the victims without questions.

When news of a disaster reached the New York office, staff immediately sprang into action. They were able to send helicopters to areas where road access was limited. As often as she could, Ms. Layug would be there with other workers. When other NGOs arrived, the staff of the Global Foundation would leave and let others carry on their good deeds. The Global Foundation network was a close-knit and efficient worldwide network. It could function due to its vast resources and connections—with not only local NGOs but also with many volunteers who could be called up at the shortest notice by phone, email, or Morse code in places where no computer communication satellites were available.

Such an instant capability for relief work created a strong imprint on the reputation of the Global Foundation. Printed on the envelopes containing emergency money for the victims were just the address, phone number, and email address of the Global Foundation. Many victims lived in well-to-do regions; they later actually donated back more than they received from the Foundation.

The real reason for the Global Foundation's existence was the dream of a few with a vision of world peace. The charity function was just a façade to cover up the real goal—peace without bullets, a new world order.

FOOTBALL WEEKENDS

The Neyland Stadium in Knoxville, Tennessee has been the home of the football team of the University of Tennessee Volunteers. According to football writers, Neyland Stadium and Knoxville has the best football weekends in the US.

The stadium was first named Shield-Watkins Field in 1921 with a capacity of 3,200. Later it was renamed Neyland Stadium because of the contribution by General Neyland who was also a head football coach. With periodical additions, modifications and modernizations, the capacity reached 102,455 seats. The surface was at first natural grass, then artificial turf, then back to natural grass to minimize injuries. It became the sixth largest football stadium in the world. During off seasons it has been used for various purposes, from rock concerts to religious functions. In May of 1970, just weeks after the shooting by the Ohio National Guard of students protesting against the Vietnam War at Kent State University, evangelist Billy Graham, with President Nixon as a guest speaker, filled the stadium to capacity.

On any football Saturday, rain or shine, one can hear the roar of the audience miles away from the stadium, across the Tennessee River to the agricultural campus of the University of Tennessee. If one could capture and transform this sound energy into potential energy in the form of propellant fuel, the quantity could have sent a man to the moon and back!

The student section in the stadium was on the east side, left of the fifty-yard line. This section was always overfilled. Students always spilled over to other sections. Within this student section one could always find some thirty graduate students of biological sciences sitting in two rows cheering just like other students. They yelled and jumped up and down, some with oranges with an alcohol infusion of one kind or another. Even the most conservative, studious graduate students would behave like undergraduates.

Among these graduate students, there were seven buddies at various stages of their graduate training, some four or five years apart. They shared most of their course work, and did their dissertation research either together in the same laboratory or in different laboratories under the guidance of the same or different professors. There was one common denominator—they were all involved in the cutting edge molecular biology and nanotechnology, working with different model systems.

They called themselves "Volunteer buddies," or "the seven Vols" for short. Their ages ranged from twenty-one to thirtyish.

Jack was the most senior in age and an ex-marine. His study concentrated on genetic engineering. He was usually the one from whom younger male members would seek personal advice.

John was the most advanced in his dissertation research and expected to graduate within a year. He already had a job lined up in a big pharmaceutical firm in charge of R&D drug delivery with nano-robotic systems, or nanobots.

Jerry worked on insects and later joined the army as a physiologist in a medical unit. His wife was a school teacher who frequently came to his lab at night to keep him company.

Harold, a non-Caucasian of Chinese ethnicity, studied the hemoglobin formation using chick embryos as a model system. He would scribble his scientific ideas on the blackboard, and propose theories and experiments. Food was his other hobby.

Ruth was a teacher in an elementary school in a small town in Mississippi. She had decided to pursue graduate studies after ten-year tenure in teaching. She shared the laboratory and was under the guidance of the same professor as Jerry. Young female graduate students would seek her advice on personal problems.

Jim, like Ruth, gave up his high-school teaching to pursue graduate studies. He worked on insect development under a different professor of entomology than Ruth and Jerry. Jim's wife worked in a bank. On holidays such as Thanksgiving, when many single people did not go home, they would cook dinner for them.

June was the youngest and a freshman graduate student working on hormone systems in newborn rats. By public proclamation, she was the most beautiful woman in the graduate school. She could compete with any Hollywood starlet. She was also the most organized and efficient individual among these seven Vol buddies.

There was "on and off short-term" romance among these seven buddies to break up the monotony of laboratory grinds. After all, they saw each other almost daily, and at times worked into the early morning together. They all went their separate ways after graduation. June was the only one without a family after her twice-failed marriage. They kept in contact and shared the joy of their families at a sort of reunion from time to time. Because of their research endeavors they shared the same common goal, i.e. molecular therapy at the level of genes and delivery systems, so they often met at the same scientific conferences. Those too were reunions of a sort.

MYSTERIOUS DEATH

The Ebola virus was an epidemic in the year of 2014 and 2015. A couple of years later it was under control because a vaccine had been developed. Immunization of a vast number of Africans and those who worked in Africa had reduced the Ebola infection to the level of the malaria infection, near zero. The Zika virus was the cause of many deformed newborns starting in 2016. That too was virtually eliminated in a year. The whole world including Africa and the Amazon was in good health, with no epidemics like Ebola or Zika for years. With the help of industrial countries, especially China, the economy in these so-called third-world countries had rapidly kept up with the rest of the world. Soon there would be no more third-world countries. Due to the conscience of modern society, there were still pockets of natives deep in the vast rain forest of the Amazon untouched by the modern world. They were left alone, some with our knowledge and some without.

Westerners like Henry Ford tried to use the rich resources in the Amazon to benefit their products, tires for cars, by clear-cutting to transform large areas of the rain forest into rubber-tree plantations. Not knowing the nature of the rubber trees that needed a certain amount of space between them to grow well, Henry Ford failed. Dense cultivations, like those for corns and rice etc., were not possible for rubber trees. Fortunately these molested areas were small compared to the total area of the Amazon rain forest. The majority of this land was later used for cash crops like soybeans and corn.

Although the Brazilian government had done a great job to protect the wild life, there were still poachers. These poachers however did play an important dualistic role. They would accidentally discover small tribes untouched by the modern world. Their discovery at times would be reported to the government. That information was important in an attempt to keep the indigenous in a virgin state in the Amazon.

On a particular day, several poachers discovered the complete death— from babies to the elderly—of a small village with approximately a hundred people, deep in the Amazon rain forest. Poachers were very alert and very "Amazon smart" to stay clear of this small area. They took pictures and reported what they observed to the appropriate authority in Manaus, the biggest city in the Amazon. Officials knew they were poachers. Because of the lack of evidence officials could not prosecute them. On the contrary, officials at times would seek information from the poachers on conditions of the Amazon. It was a give and take that benefited both sides of the law.

After getting the news of this unusual, strange death in a remote area of the Amazon from the poachers, officials immediately sprang into action. Since the poachers had not entered the area or touched anything there, their possible contribution to the deaths was eliminated. The poachers were also healthy. A special recovery team was sent to collect bodies which they bagged and stored in isolated refrigerated morgues in Manaus for autopsies and examination by medical and scientific personnel. The rest of the dead were buried immediately on site. All the personnel in this unpleasant task wore spacesuit-like clothing to protect themselves as well as prevent contamination to and from the outside world.

Experts—from the United Nations Special Medical Corp, US Center for Disease Control (CDC), Brazilian CDC, European Center for Disease Prevention and Control (ECDPC), plus the most elite group of anti-bioterrorists from Israel—used the most sophisticated instruments yet found no definitive answers as to how or why every individual in a whole village had died. People appeared to have died within a short time, maybe within hours. Tissue samples and autopsies revealed no known or unknown infectious agents from the modern world.

Electron microscope examinations revealed no viral particles in the tissue samples. Antigen-antibody reactions revealed no known disease agents in the tissue fluid, from viral to bacterial infections known to every corner of the world. Tissues samples including blood and lymph fluid appeared normal. There was no evidence of autoimmune reactions.

All the deaths, from babies to the elderly, appeared to result from the same unknown cause or causes. There was no evidence that the villagers knew what had happened. One of the pictures taken by the poachers showed a young mother nursing a baby who died with a smile on her face! Playing children had just laid down and died. There were no stressful expressions on their faces.

Did they die in good health?

Other than the poachers, who were at a safe distant from the village, they appeared to have no contact with the outside world. The only other remote physical contact, if any, was a low-flying prop plane owned by the Global Foundation. It had flown to Manaus from Rio de Janeiro over the location of this "death village" on the way back from helping the victims, mostly tourists, of a sudden volcano eruption on a small island ten miles outside Rio de Janeiro. The eruption was small, so was the island. As usual, when governmental agencies or NGOs like the Red Cross arrived, the Global Foundation personnel had left and let the big agencies take care of the long-term rescue and recovery tasks.

Two weeks before the strange death of this remote village in the Amazon, hundreds of dead hyenas were discovered at a watering site in the Serengeti, where a sanctuary of wildlife was located with support from the UN and several NGOs, including the Global Foundation. Other animals were fine with no unusual death or sickness. Death came only to the hyenas—not the lions, not the zebras, not the deer and other animals that shared the watering hole. The hyenas appeared to just lie down and die. There was no sign of infection of any kind. Regular tests and autopsies done on dead animals in the sanctuary revealed no unusual or usual cause of death.

The death of the animals did not generate excitement in the general public news media. However, wildlife experts and veterinarians were puzzled. Weeks later, health experts of both humans and animals, began to suspect a similarity between the death of the hyenas and the people in the village in the Amazon. These two seemingly unrelated events did arouse notice in the news media.

Since all of the examinations of frozen samples by the most elite institutions in the world yielded negative results, i.e. no known cause of death, soon the world forgot about them.

The world continued as usual, including multiple killings of innocent people because leaders started wars on the pretext of peace. In addition, they thought war was good for their people, their economies, and most important of all, for filling the pockets of the makers of war machines and bullets. Almost every leader in the world had connections, big or small, with these instruments of death that they used in the name of peace and at the cost of thousands of innocent lives.

THREE YEARS AGO

Three years ago, Mr. Erikson, Ms. Layug, and Mr. Kennedy met in a room in the basement of the Global Foundation in Manhattan with the board members, including successful industrialists, financial mogul, real estate, and scientists. Not only was the room soundproof, every inch in the wall was copper wired, including the ceiling and the floor. It was like a Faraday cage where no electronic and sound waves could penetrate in or out.

The board members were: DJ Chu of Beijing, who owned the largest construction firm in the world (ironically his firm was subsidized by the government); Ms. Jankovic of Serbia who owned the Trans-Siberian Railroad in addition to many other transportation companies; Dr. John Jones, one of the seven Tennessee graduate students, who was a VP of R&D in the US of the largest pharmaceutical firm in the world, AZ, Inc.; Dr. Rogers who was a Nobel Laureate and professor of microbiology at Harvard; Mr. W. Shum of Hong Kong who owned hundreds of hotels around the world; Mr. Sonnovovitch of Russia who was a member of the Politburo; and Prof. Alvarado of Brazil who was the Director of Amazon Conservation (a quasi-government organization). These people were the core members of the board.

There was no recording device. Mr. Triple E opened the meeting without wasting words, just, "Welcome, be comfortable. We shall end when we need to end."

After all the customary greetings and the servers had left, Mr. Erikson took the floor. "Six years ago, we met at one of UNESCO's annual dinners. Some of you may have known each other then. I was chairing UNESCO, I knew some of you and others by reputation, and read about you so I could do my job. Somehow we all sort of met in the corridor during a break and started to talk, actually it was my job to do PR. From the beginning we hit it off and decided to have dinner together. From then on, we have had many informal and, like today, formal meetings. We share a common notion that the existing world will gradually deteriorate into an abyss. Leaders of the world have the universal perception that winning wars are good for their countries. Leaders want wars in order to have peace, so they profess. They think war is a natural providence of mankind. The result has been the killing of many innocent people, nicely termed as collateral damage. Six years ago we all agreed that a new world order is needed. That started our "universal perception" that pursuing peace would be our goal. Gradually we formulated a workable approach to gain peace without bullets. In the intervening years, we have accumulated enough resources to begin. Thus we are here today. It is time to begin."

They wasted no time. The second speaker was Mr. Kennedy whose report was short and sweet. "We have 300 billion US dollars, about 500 RMB, and equal amount of Euros, a little over one trillion in total. I have put aside twenty percent as an emergency fund. The rest can be used immediately for operations. The money is in various banks, your firms, and private accounts. Thank you to all of you here who have been accumulating since the onset by the Global Foundation some six years ago."

Every face in the room carried a positive smile.

The next speaker was Ms. Layug. She wore a conservative, designer dress and stood 5'6" without heels. Her voice was gentle, with a certain firmness that could pacify any angry crowd.

"We have plenty of operation funds for immediate rescue operations in disaster areas anywhere in the world," she said. "We have a number of capable teams for such action. Within these groups, we have identified who we can trust to lead future operations. At our next meeting they will be here. Their participation can wait until we firm up our agenda tonight or later."

Mr. Shum, a tycoon from Hong Kong in the real estate and hospitality industries spoke next. "According to our discussions last time, we need to create a specific agent unknown to present-day science. Our scientists cannot do their work in their existing laboratories. We need a laboratory isolated from all civilization, known to no one except us and the necessary personnel like our chief scientists and their trusted associates. Not even the supporting staff must know where they are. I believe this should be our first priority."

"And the construction time line should be as short as possible," added Mr. DJ Chu. He liked to be called DJ and was the owner of the largest construction firm in the world.

"Yes," echoed the others.

"The location should be in an environment that would be convenient enough because there will initially be much transportation of personnel and equipment. Periodic trips in and out, like vacations, will certainly be needed," said Ms. Jankovic from Serbia.

Ms. Jankovic was Secretary of Transportation as well as the richest person in Serbia. She had inherited from her father a fortune in domestic air and rail transport business. She was able to expand internationally with holdings of many international transportation businesses including the Trans-Siberian Railroad. She sat on many boards. She would later handle all the transportation matters for the ambitious project of the Global Foundation.

The tall gentleman with salt-pepper hair from Moscow raised his head and gestured for others to listen—Mr. Sonnovovitch had been in the Moscow military academy in his younger days. "I believe we have a perfect site for the laboratory. During the cold war with America, we built many bomb shelters in case there was an outright nuclear war. None of them were put to use as we had no wars. Many of them have been forgotten. I have inherited the job in charge of their locations and readiness, just in case. There is one site that is ideal for us in the middle of Siberia. The shelter can house 50 to 400. I think all the facilities are still functioning like the ventilation, living quarters, etc. We, or some of us, can go there to ascertain the situation. I will be with them, I know exactly where it is. We use a railway station in the middle of Siberia as an entrance for that bomb shelter. One of the two tracks in front of the station is probably rusty. The other track is part of the Trans-Siberian Railroad from Moscow to the city of Vladivostok. Let us visit that site as soon as possible. Ms. Jankovic owns that railroad."

Mr. Triple E looked at Ms. Jankovic and Ms. Layug, and asked: "How soon can transportation be arranged?"

Mr. Shum replied, "We have to transform ourselves as tourists therefore not arousing suspicions to visit such a dissolute location in the middle of nowhere. Or as an exploration team? We cannot just ask the train master to stop there and let us off."

"I can arrange that," said Ms. Jankovic from Serbia. "We can travel to Vladivostok. From there, we can fly to that location, can't we? There is an airport or airstrip, right?"

"There is a rough airstrip for small planes. We can check the satellite to see if we can spot it again," Mr. Sonnovovitch said. "If it is still there, maybe we can find an old plane flying from Vladivostok. We have to be discreet or even act in secrecy—Russia is still pretty sensitive about foreign visitors to Siberia because there is much to be explored for the rich resources underground."

"Maybe we can create a small disaster. Is there a small town within driving distance from this abandoned rail station?" asked Ms. Jankovic.

"Yes," replied Mr. Sonnovovitch, "there is a mining town, Suntar, about thirty kilometers from the station. There is a small airport, just a landing strip. There is no more mining, and no miners now. They all became tourist guides for foreigners going hunting and fishing in the summer. In the winter, the town literally shuts down and everyone either goes to Moscow, Vladivostok, or just stays inside watching TV. There are less than a hundred or so who stay put. At times rich foreigners want to experience what a severe winter is like. And there are winter sports such as hunting polar bears, and dog sled rides for rich Americans, oil cartels, and Chinese. I am sure the people in Suntar have a few tour buses."

"Perfect," said Dr. Rogers from Harvard. "I can culture some little known but not virulent microbes. Next winter, which is just around the corner, we can find a way to infect the residents to create a small disaster there. However, in winter not many rescuers will arrive within a short time. That may pose a problem."

"I think it can be done, quite easily too," said Mr. Kennedy. "We have a twin turboprop in Tianjin, China. We lease it to either the Chinese or Japanese or people in Vladivostok if they need it for short distances. We can use the plane to fly to Suntar as a team and travel to the abandoned station. Is there a name?"

"Just a number, Shelter 113. And for security we did not even register it as a rail station," replied the Russian.

"I can arrange appropriate transportation to that shelter," said Ms. Jankovic. "I have a very trusted member of staff in Vladivostok keeping an eye on my operation there. He can go with the group as a tour guide, drive a small tour bus from Suntar with all the tourist gear, fishing poles, etc. Or we can all be disguised as rescue workers. Mr. Sonnovovitch, do you know the entrance, which is probably secret too?"

"No, but I can certainly find out from our, i.e. my, file. I have deleted some of the site information from the official records kept in Moscow just in case we need it to be gone. Now it meets our need and is convenient."

With the physical needs of the laboratory out of the way, the board turned to the most difficult task of sacrificing animals and humans in order to achieve their ultimate goal.

"We need to identify target populations, both animals and humans as a warning, so-called sacrificial lambs, so the warring nations can heed our threat for their safety and their lives," said Mr. Erikson with a grim expression.

On that topic of sacrificial lambs, the Global Foundation board had labored and agonized for weeks, both individually and in groups because it involved the taking of innocent human and animal lives. The latter was easy because there were animals like hyenas that were not on the endangered list.

Peace without guns and bullets. Peace by the oldest means, sacrifice.

Mr. Erikson answered the question on every board member's mind. "To sacrifice a few in order to save thousands may be an antithesis of our peace formula. To end the World War II, the US decided to drop the atomic bombs to save many innocent lives. If we accept this as a legitimate means of action, it may be easier on our conscience."

The room was silent for a couple of minutes. Nevertheless, all the board members realized that a human sacrifice would elicit the greatest reactions from the warring leaders.

"There are numerous small tribes deep in the Amazon. My job includes knowing many poachers. They serve as valuable informants to tell us the locations and the welfare of these "lost tribes." Their locations can be precisely pinpointed with the GPSs that I gave them. I can contact the poachers, a secret that neither you nor the government of Brazil need to know, when I get back to Manaus," said Prof. Alvarado.

DIVERSION WITH A SMALL DISASTER

Three weeks after the Manhattan meeting, a small town named Suntar in Siberia was shutting down for the winter. The Trans-Siberian Railroad would make several five-minute stops here before the severe Siberia winter set in, to pick up passengers who would spend their winter in warmer places. The lonely station manager would stay to collect the mail for whoever stayed in town. If there were no passengers, the train just slowed down and the mail and any other deliveries were thrown onto the platform, and any outbound parcels were handed to the train conductor.

On one eastbound train a mail pouch was dropped. One of the small boxes with an address to the one and only store was delivered to that address by the railroad station manager who doubled as the postmaster. In the winter time this general store was the town center for those who opted to stay (less than fifty). Inside the wrapping paper was a thin layer of powder the color of the wrapping paper. This powder was what Prof. Rogers at Harvard was referring to in that Manhattan meeting—the infectious but harmless microbes.

Within forty-eight hours, almost everyone in Suntar developed a strange rash on their bodies and a mild fever. An immediate alert for help was sent to the closest city, Vladivostok. The operator for Ms. Jankovic was one of the city council members who received that urgent message. He at once called DJ, i.e. Mr. Chu, in Beijing. The Global Foundation offered a plane from Tianjin to Vladivostok and on to Suntar to ferry their workers and medical supplies. Among the rescue workers were Mr. Sonnovovitch, Mr. Chuen Lo, Ms. Jankovic, and a few other Global Foundation members of staff.

Mr. Chuen Lo was a known crackpot civil engineer who took on many projects that no other civil engineers would touch. He had been recruited to the inner circle of the Global Foundation by Ms. Paz Layug who knew his wife. The ladies were from the Philippines and they had attended high school and college together.

After landing in Suntar, these few Global Foundation personnel drove to Shelter 113 in a minibus that belonged to one of the winter residents. The residents in Suntar did not bother with this operation because they were all sick at home, and the pot-holed landing strip was several kilometers from town.

With just general antibiotics carried by the "rescue workers," the Global Foundation staff headed to Suntar, and the rash was cured within two weeks. No one died.

This was a good trial run as an alternative means of transportation just in case the movable track platform malfunctioned or was rendered nonfunctional by accident. At least an evacuation of personnel could be accomplished if needed. That was the brain child of Mr. Sonnovovitch, ex-KGB.

Mr. Sonnovovitch, DJ, and Mr. Chuen Lo checked out Shelter 113. They flipped switches, checked petroleum tanks, turned ventilation vents on and off, and checked every storage cabinet and facility. Although the shelter had not been used, almost all equipment was still in working order. The canned food was still good; nothing had spoiled at the constant temperature and humidity. This underground shelter was in excellent shape.

"It won't take much modification to make it into a functional—albeit not luxury—building with a laboratory and residence. The ventilation is still working well. That is important. I would say three months top," said Mr. Chuen Lo.

"I will take care of the workers and supplies," said DJ. "Mr. Sonnovovitch, we will need you to take care of the politics or diplomacy if needed to cover up our work, while Ms. Jankovic will take care of the transport. How many workers will you need, Mr. Chuen Lo?"

"Ten, with supplies for living underground until the laboratories are finished."

"One of the designs of many shelters was an elevator in addition to stairs," said Mr. Sonnovovitch. "Many sections of the entire track at different locations along the Trans-Siberian Railway were designed to be able to disengage easily so the Americans would not be able to use it if they captured it. The foundation of a section at the station, a length of a rail car, was also designed to be a platform, like the stage in a theater but more formidable. The elevator can handle a missile launcher."

After looking over the platform, Mr. Chuen Lo said: "It would not be difficult to modify this track platform and enlarge the existing tunnel connecting our laboratory. The whole car can be lowered with all the supplies and people inside as one unit. I think my staff can accomplish this and modify the interior into living quarters within three months. Since it is underground, it will not be discovered easily. The challenge is to transport all the required equipment and personnel in secrecy."

"I will handle these details," said Ms. Jankovic, who was supposed to be a nurse on the rescue team, and had disappeared with the other rescuers after arriving at Suntar. "I will designate some of my staff to replace the regular drivers as required. In our firm, we frequently surprise employees by giving them special vacations because of their meritorious performance—a Singapore model."

The chief architect for laboratory design was Ms. Lorraine who had designed many laboratories for universities and industries. It was the most difficult assignment that she ever had. On the other hand it was easy because of the secrecy. Since it was virtually a closed system, designing a level-4 microbiological laboratory needed special equipment, ventilation, and air filtration systems. Most of the crew hired for construction would stay after the completion as maintenance personnel for three years. They were the best building engineers and construction crew that money could buy. And they would be rewarded with an amount equivalent to what they would otherwise earn by working regularly up until their retirement. They were all Chinese from DJ's construction empire.

The location of the laboratory was ideal because of its isolation from major population centers. And, most importantly, satellites from the USA, France, Japan, and Great Britain rarely flew over this desolate region. Within three months the physical portion of the laboratory and scientific personnel were set up and running. Transportation to and from the laboratory via the Trans-Siberian train was in place to begin the operation toward peace without bullets.

REUNION OF THE SEVEN VOLS

In May, the largest and most influential scientific conference on molecular therapy was held in London. Many new discoveries and technological advances would be discussed in this four-day period. Industrialists and scientists formed small discussion groups on how best to use these discoveries. It was just another international sci-tech meeting, except there was a hidden agenda, an agenda that involved only seven scientists.

A week before the meeting in London, each of the graduate student buddies who had studied at the University of Tennessee received a call from John, the most senior when they were at graduate school. John wanted everyone to go to the conference for a "special reunion."

Since their graduation over twenty years ago, the seven Vol buddies had all gone separate ways at different institutions. Each of them had gained an admirable reputation in their own R&D or professorial posts. Some had families.

John had a large suite at a hotel near the Marble Arch. The other six Volunteer buddies were staying at different hotels nearby. On the second day of the conference the Vols, plus a fifteen-year-old young woman, Alex, met in John's suite.

After the greetings, hugs, and small talk about families, they got down to business.

Looking at everyone, John spoke in a most serious manner: "Thank you for leaving your regular duties and families to come on such a short notice. And I'd like to introduce Alex who has been working with me for a couple years in our Program for Young Scientists. She is the best DNA chemist I know."

John paused for a few seconds. "I have undertaken a very difficult task. And the task has to be discreet, actually secret. I need all your talent and expertise. And I trust your discretion. After I disclose what the task ahead is, you don't have to participate. I trust you and value our friendship and comradeship from day one of our graduate study days."

"OK, John, let's have it," said Harold.

"About six years ago, several industrialists and academicians met in a corridor at the United Nations for a UNESCO annual meeting. To make a long story short, we hit it off so well that dinners and meeting were to follow for several years with the same members. Our consensus was that a new world order was needed. Since the end of World War II, there have been continuous wars and battles, large and small, killing millions of innocent people of all ages. World leaders go to war because they think wars, especially winning them, are good for the country, pride, economy, world status, and other reasons. The new world order we discussed was peace. Unlike the world leaders' thoughts of wars with bullets and missiles for peace, some said, we have been discussing peace without bullets.

"We also realized that what we had in mind was a two-edged sword. How does one achieve peace without bullets? I have been thinking about using our expertise in molecular biology and its application to molecular therapy. We will develop methods targeting a particular gene or genes to annihilate a certain population of animals. Their death will be followed by that of a small human population, as sacrificial lambs so to speak, to show world leaders we have the means to target them as well if they do not stop fighting. Our demand and reward will be an end to war and the elimination of all war-making machines, and we hold the trump cards."

After this lengthy opening statement from John, the others looked at each other with puzzled expressions.

"John," said Alex, "I am going to play my video games next door while you adults talk, OK?"

"Go ahead."

"John," June asked, "I still don't understand the role we will play in this scheme, program, or whatever you mean by a new world order."

"Peace without bullets?" queried Jack.

"Germ warfare or something like that?" asked Jim.

"That is still war, John," said Ruth.

"Terrorism?" asked June, alarmed.

"A biological warfare with specific targets," said John.

"What targets are you talking about?" asked Harold.

"We will target a particular gene or genes in a population or individuals. This is not specifically germ warfare as we commonly conceptualize it. As I said, this method of warfare, discussed and supported by a group of non-scientist backers, is a double-edged sword. If our means fell into the wrong hands it would be the beginning of the end of humanity."

"A double-edged sword!" Jim exclaimed. "Killing certain animal species and a small population of people will be our warning signals?"

"Precisely," said John. "This is a tremendous sacrifice and risk. With that said, we all go back a long way and we trust each other with our lives. However, the risk and the scheme of 'peace without bullets' may not be uniform in our minds. I think you understand what I am driving at."

The other six buddies looked at John and each other, concern written on every face. They all now realized the purpose of this gathering.

John continued, "I know each of you and we know each other very well; in some ways better than our families. If you want to withdraw from this scheme, please do so. And I trust you not to breathe a word about this meeting."

"I am in." All the Vols seemed to speak in unison, like cheering a touch-down against Alabama.

"Several of us who share the same convictions have been talking for several years," said John. "We have been discussing the means to achieve peace without bullets. There are about ten leaders in the business world, from real estate to pharmaceuticals. You will meet them later. The backers have agreed and I was hoping you would join us. I am one of the original 'instigators.' The reason for secrecy is so as not to arouse public curiosity or suspicion by world leaders. As you know, they and their governments are always leery about charity foundations including the Red Cross. I am sorry that it looks like a cloak-and-dagger game. I know you know why. I will give you instructions to meet with the support members in New York."

"I love to play spy games!" said Jerry. "I have been in the army long enough. I could wear all my medals on my uniform walking in. How's that, John?"

"Just say the word. I have been in the Pentagon too," said Jack.

"Hey, how about the rest of us civilians?" asked Harold.

"Guys, we have had enough for today. Breakfast tomorrow here," said John, wrapping up the meeting.

Harold and June eyed each other and left together.

John's wife, Rita, came in to fetch Alex and take her shopping.

To Die in Good Health

The next morning, the seven Vol buddies met again in John's suite after breakfast. They came in at different times, in pairs and individually.

John addressed them: "We had our great reunion yesterday, just as all other reunions. In addition to what we discussed yesterday, I'd like to reiterate: Our approach to a new world order could be interpreted as a terrorist act because we will have to sacrifice a small number of human beings and a couple of populations of animals to show the world leaders how we can target selected individuals at will. We will show them all—the leaders, premiers, presidents, all of them—what we can do. Now, if you have any doubt or are bothered by our approach, you can still back out. If so, I still place trust in our friendship that you will keep this information; and our meetings never happened, as the cliché goes."

Without so many words, the Vol buddies all decided to stay in.

"We all have our own labs and associates. How, where, and what we will do without others knowing?" asked Harold.

"I too assume all the future work related to this 'peace without bullets' project will be in secrecy, if not total secrecy," added June.

"Yes. Total secrecy," replied John.

"What about the logistics?" asked Jack.

"I assume we have to work in some lab somewhere, but not ours?" inquired Ruth.

"Yes, Ruth," continued John. "We have identified a location for a laboratory to undertake this project. The lab will be in the middle of Siberia. No, we will not do our work there. We will send our most capable associates there in secret, and persuade them to spend three years, or less I hope, in isolation to accomplish the task ahead. We will communicate with each other through codes, encrypted emails, and other clandestine methods."

"Wow!" exclaimed Jerry.

"Guys, that is why I asked you all here. Trusting one another and our friendship is of the utmost importance to keep our project undetected and unknown to other scientific communities, including many of our colleagues and collaborators. To be successful, they are NOT TO KNOW, in capital letters!"

"One suggestion, John, you may have thought about it," said Jack. "That is, our associates will have their own tasks, separate tasks, experiments etc. We shall collate the data. That is a precaution to maintain secrecy."

"We shall communicate with codes, it is necessary," added Jerry.

"Well said, you two," said John.

"I think, John, we committed ourselves when we came here for breakfast today," said Jim. "What do you have in mind for us to do, John?"

"The first task is for us to develop, invent or create an agent—biological or synthetic—to annihilate or target a small population of human and animals without harming others in the vicinity or in a dense population."

"Targeting a particular gene or genes or gene products?" asked Jack.

"That would be very specifically target-oriented," replied Jim.

Jim was working on the control, but not elimination, of a few species of harmful insects to farm products in Asia. His targets were at the DNA level—precisely, particular short sequences that control the expression of genes. It was a matter of transferring the methodology to other organisms including human; it would be possible but not easy. That actually would be Jim's major contribution to the project.

"If I may, and please keep this within these walls," said Jack, "At the Pentagon we are actually doing precisely what Jim is doing with insects, but with cultured human cells. As you know, those of us who work in the governmental service work 9 to 5. Only a handful of people will work before or after hours, and we work only five days a week. Eventually we will finish, but by that time the private sector will be far ahead of us. Who takes the credit? We do. We stake our claim under the umbrella of national security. We are powerful enough to persuade companies in the private sector to keep quiet, sometimes we pay them for their effort."

"I should have worked with you, Jack, my ex-roommate," smiled Harold.

"Knowing you, Harold, you would be bored to death," retorted June. "You have no patience to wait for others whose work may be supplemental or complement your own."

June and Harold had been office mates for several years in Knoxville. They had got to know each other very well and developed more than just an office-sharing relationship. Harold had his family after graduation. He had been a widower for a few years. June was again single after two failed marriages.

John continued, "Jack and Jerry are not civilians. They know their way around the government. You two will help us form a wall around our project. In other words, I am asking you to cheat for us. And to find out what agency or agencies are doing that is related to our work. Jack mentioned that earlier. And although government lab work is slow, they do not lack talented scientists. Some of them are as dedicated as we are. They like their 'iron bowl' jobs, mostly for the security of their families.

"We in private sector are never 100% secure. In industries like my firm, orders come from the top. We have to convince the corporate division which research will be a financial advantage over our competitors. So far, I have been winning. You in academia, like Harold, June, Jim and Ruth, have a lot freedom to pursue your own ideas. You don't need to follow directives or guidelines. Lucky you!"

"Right, John, that is academic freedom," said Jim. "But our grants cannot afford this suite." He was echoed by June, Harold and Ruth. "Of course, we are by no means poor. We are comfortable, so are our families."

"Ok, let us get back on track," said Jerry.

"So, first we will develop an agent or agents targeting particular gene or genes," said John. "And it should not be detectable, i.e. it must self-destruct afterward. We may be able to extend from the CRISPR technology. By the way, Dr. Rogers of Harvard, I think you know of him, is one of the supporting members. He and I had long talk about this before I approached you guys."

"I think the target or targets should be scattered in the genome so that no single gene or a group of genes will stand out as being affected," said Ruth.

"Jerry, aren't you working on a certain expression in the Krebs cycle?" asked Harold.

"Yes," Jerry replied. "We want to slow down the biochemical process, not blocking it out completely. The end result, we hope, will be to decrease the combat ability of field soldiers. Make them lazy."

"Make them relax, happy, and just go," said Alex, the fifteen-year-old genius walking in with her favorite orange lollipop. "They will quietly die not knowing what happened. If there is such a thing as dying happy, this is it."

"Alex, did you overhear our conversation?" asked John.

"Yes, the door was open. I was playing this video game. They shoot each other, not with bullets, but with a hypothetical 'void' energy, particles without mass. When I heard Krebs cycle, I shifted my attention to your conversation. Of course, John, I will never tell anyone. Besides, my contemporaries have a difficult time understanding me when I talk science."

After the morning discussions of the feasibility to develop such an agent or agents, they broke for lunch. In order not to raise attention by others in the conference, industry spies, and government agents, they went out at different times and went to different places for lunch. Rita, John's wife, took Alex shopping.

SWARMING NANOBOTS

Having decided to target genes controlling the biochemical processes that generated energy in the Krebs cycle, the seven Vol buddies decided to have synthetic short DNA nucleotides affecting these genes. The shorter the nucleotides the easier to synthesize—as well as breaking up into mononucleotides, the building blocks of DNA—back into the pool in the living cells. The task was to synthesize the nucleotides that could bind to the controlling sequence(s) that produced energy as well as those that utilized a carbon-based energy source within a certain population or individuals.

The next task was how to deliver the final product. A random delivery system, like a spray to disperse the agent or agents, was ruled out because they could not target a particular population or individuals in a population. The effecting nucleotides must be in some aggregate form or encapsulated to get around such randomness. Encapsulation was easiest because the technology had been around since mid-twentieth century. However, the delivery of encapsulated nucleotides to a particular site in which the targeted organism was located was not an easy task.

With an armful of shopping bags, Alex walked in just in time to hear the conversation. She looked at her purchases and opened a few wrapped items.

"How about robots?" she said.

Everyone turned their head and looked at Alex with admiration.

"Thanks, Alex," said John. "Nanobots. In AZ Pharm we are working on drug delivery systems with nanobots instead of an injection of liquid or embedding solids. Nanobots can be made to have affinity to specific tissue or cells. They can travel in the blood stream until they find their target."

"For an injection, that is fine. But we cannot just poke needles in everyone regardless if our bullets are encapsulated or carried by nanobots," countered June.

"Nor we can embed the nucleotides in sugar cubes like the Sabin vaccine feeding them to a population," added Jim.

"Air drop. With a specific guidance system or affinity for the targets," Alex said.

"Why didn't we think of that?" Jack looked at Alex and gave her a thumb up.

Ruth looked thoughtful. "If we are dealing with a population, regardless how big or small, the nanobots cannot be scattered by the wind. Even in a closed environment, there is always a current. And it does not take much to scatter the nanobots. They are not insects that can swarm like bees heading out to seek nectar in a sunflower patch."

"We can use nanobots as carriers for the encapsulated nucleotide agents," suggested John, "then program them to be able to swarm into a population, as Ruth said about bees. Can we program them to seek out selected targets in a mixed population?"

"May I make a preliminary conclusion?" asked Harold.

"Go ahead," said John, nodding.

"We need to synthesis short DNA or RNA, nucleotide sequences that can bind, modify, or prevent expression of genes in the Krebs cycle. But they cannot completely inhibit their normal function. Just slow them down. Encapsulate these nucleotides. We shall develop specific nanobots that have the property of swarming and selectively go to a target organism in a mixed population."

John wrapped up the meeting. "Guys, we have accomplished a lot in these two days. Now is the time to finalize our protocol for a new world order when we go back. I have arranged for all of us to meet the major players who support our science and bring it to fruition. Peace without bullets."

"John, you have not told us who the makers and shakers are," said Jack.

"No, but I will tell you now. Are you familiar with the Global Foundation?"

"Isn't it a charity like the Catholic Foundation, Presbyterian Foundation, and the Red Cross, i.e. NGOs that help victims from both natural and man-made disasters?"

"Yes. One and the same." John nodded. "The Global Foundation does do what the Red Cross and other NGOs do with the same percept. Except, we—I mean the Global Foundation—have not been satisfied with just rescue missions. We want to have sustainable peace, no war, no collateral damage, i.e. no more mass killing of innocent people."

John continued to inform his buddy Vols in detail the history on how the idea was first conceived. He proceeded to tell others the identity of the founding members.

"I took the liberty of asking you all here, and of arranging a meeting with the founding members of the Global Foundation. I was one of them. Dr. Rogers, a Nobel Laureate you know, is another scientist. There is a Volunteer Day in the Global Foundation in Manhattan. We do this once or twice a year to appreciate the work of our volunteers. We open the door, invite them in to talk to our officers and board members. They can stay as long as they want, enjoy refreshments, and view videos of our rescue missions. There is some light entertainment, a quartet, and light jazz to make them feel at home. Make them part of us. At that time we will have a formal meeting with our board members. We will discuss how we can support your work and keep it secret too."

"I assume we have to be discreet. Not being a spook, how do we do that?" asked June.

"Yes, more than discreet. Your visit to the Global Foundation will not be known to any person, government, or NGO—only to the Global Foundation board members. Therefore it will be like a clandestine operation. I already talked to Jack and Jerry about it while you guys were having lunch.

"Why do we need to do this?" he continued. "Since 9/11 in 2001, US security agencies—more than ten of them—have been extremely cautious about any organizations, especially religious ones. It has been very difficult for nonprofit groups to apply for tax exempt status. Applicant organizations are under most detailed scrutiny. The Red Cross, the American Cancer Society and the like are being watched too. As Jack and Jerry know, other than regular surveillance cameras on street corners, additional surveillance cameras and other monitoring devices are installed whenever there is a sizable meeting, such as this Molecular Therapeutic Conference. I am quite sure that extra surveillance equipment will be installed around the Global Foundation building on the day of our Volunteer Day. Who goes in and who comes out will be known. Folders of all of you are somewhere in a government basement. You will be recognized. Just in case anyone asks what all these scientists are doing here, we have devised, with Jack and Jerry's expertise, a somewhat clandestine means for you to come in."

"I will dress like a homeless person," giggled Ruth.

"I will be a transgender person," said Harold jokingly.

"OK, guys," said John, suppressing a smile. "Jack and Jerry are in the military. They will be formally invited as our VIP guests with medals on their uniforms. They will spend some time with the volunteers. It will be advertised as our public relations job. Governments, especially national security agencies, like to get involved with private organizations like ours. No problem there."

Ruth asked, "And us civilians?"

"Jim, June, Ruth, and Harold will come early, entering through the back door. We will turn off our surveillance cameras when you come in. That will take no more than a few seconds. However, I am sure the City of New York, or other security agency, will also have installed theirs so they can record who is coming and going and the time. To bypass that, you will have to come early, before the door is opened, through the delivery entrance in the back. Sorry. But you can dress however you like. I am one of the trustees of the Foundation—no problem here or for any of our founding members, they are all well-known philanthropists from different parts of the world. You will meet them. Since a Volunteer Day is not a board meeting, it will be unusual if all of them come. Therefore, some of them will also come early like June, Jerry, Jim, and Harold."

VOLUNTEER DAY

Above the front door of the Global Foundation building hung a banner, modest but noticeable, saying *Welcome, Volunteers.* Below these words, in smaller characters were the words *9 A.M. to 5 P.M. Brunch all day.*

This was a routine way for the Foundation to thank the thousands of volunteers for their efforts. The appreciation day was held at different regions in the US as well as abroad. On this particular day, the volunteers were from the greater New York area, a mixture of all ethnicities and from all walks of life. Mr. Erikson, Ms. Layug, and other office workers mingled on and off with the volunteers throughout the day.

The Global Foundation hired the best PR firm in NYC to organize this annual event. The PR firm, headed by a charming young woman, Jewel, was always in demand. Jewel's caterer specialized in catering for charity organizations such as this. For charity organizations with numerous volunteers and contributors from one to one million or more in donations, the annual event could not be overly lavish nor just salad and cookies. It had to be just right to show the appreciation to the donors, big and small. Although Jewel had been doing this for a number of years for the Global Foundation, she did not know the nature of the Foundation other than what the public knew. It was actually better for a PR person like Jewel not to ask what her clients did.

Around 8:30 A.M., Harold, June, Jim, and Ruth arrived via the back entrance. They would meet with the members of the Global Foundation: John of AZ Pharm, Mr. Chuen Lo of NYC, Ms. Jankovic of Serbia, Mr. Kennedy of the very famous Kennedy family, Mr. DJ Chu of Beijing, Mr. Shum of Hong Kong, Ms. Layug of the Philippines, Dr. Rogers of Harvard, Mr. Erikson and Mr. Sonnovovitch of Russia. Prof. Alvarado was not able to come because of internal politics in Brazil.

After the introduction, these pioneers seeking peace without bullets started to work.

John said, "Our first step to establish a secret laboratory has been accomplished. Briefly, Mr. Sonnovovitch has provided a place, an underground shelter in the middle of Siberia, never used during the cold war era with America."

"How about lab supplies etc. How will they be transferred to the lab?" asked Harold.

Mr. Kennedy answered, "Ms. Jankovic owns the Trans-Siberian Railway. She will be responsible for that task."

"The lab?" asked June.

"I have remodeled the shelter according to standard level 4 'contamination containment' of the US-CDC guideline and the design architected by Ms. Lorraine," said Mr. Chuen Lo.

Jack asked the next question. "How did you do this without the knowledge of China, the US, Japan, Russia and other nations?"

DJ replied, "I was able to supply ten top construction workers from my firm in Beijing with all the tools. Ms. Jankovic was responsible for getting them there from Tianjin to Vladivostok then to Shelter 113."

"What, and where, is Shelter 113?" asked Ruth.

"Sorry, I have not told you about Shelter 113," said Mr. Sonnovovitch. "Shelter 113 was a bomb shelter built in the seventies during the cold war between the USSR and the USA. The Russian military built many of them in case the USA started to drop bombs, including nuclear bombs. I was responsible for the record keeping of these shelters. I was able to hide, i.e. to erase, the record of a few, just in case there was a need for them. Shelter 113 was one of these that became non-existent. It came to be useful and it is usable—the lights, ventilation, and water lines are still in good working condition. Under Mr. Chuen Lo's direction, Mr. DJ's crew has transformed the shelter into a lab with living space for fifty people, or more if necessary. When you give us a list of equipment, chemicals and other requirements, Mr. Kennedy will purchase them and Ms. Jankovic will transport them to the lab, Shelter 113."

"Sorry to ask, but how could that be accomplished considering the spying eyes of all the satellites from China, Japan, Russia, England, the USA, and the EU?" asked Jack.

"Since I own the Trans-Siberian Railway I have many trustworthy employees and colleagues working on the railroad. To minimize detection, we transport at night. It can be done from Moscow or Vladivostok," replied Ms. Jankovic. She proceeded to describe Shelter 113's location and how the last car in a long freight train would be detached and lowered into a vast underground chamber.

"But first, we will need your people to be there to receive and set up the lab," said John. "ASAP, we will need your top associates and assistants who are willing to work in isolation, with short breaks, for as long as two to three years. That is the period that I estimate will be long enough for us to perfect the methodology for our purpose."

Mr. Triple E added, "We will reward them monetarily as well as give them other physical and/or psychological support that will be sufficient for the rest of their lives. We can even change their identities legally, like the FBI does with the witness program."

"Excuse my ignorance, the Global Foundation is a NGO. How are you able to do this?" Jerry asked.

"Forgive me, ladies and gentlemen, I neglected to mention one very important element in our organization," explained Mr. Triple E. "In addition to us here—all civilians, some with government connections, like DJ of Beijing—we have involved a few powerful politicians in the US, Europe and Asia. Because of politics and their high visibility, although they share our ideology of peace, they wish to remain anonymous. I therefore cannot reveal who they are. I hope you understand. It is one of those geopolitical matters that will be beneficial to our work and to achieve our goal."

"Not being a spook or a politician, I am enlightened," said Harold looking at June, Ruth, and Jim. "Us bench scientists do have a narrow vision."

"No so, Harold," countered John. "It is just circumstantial in our profession out of our work at UNESCO. The fact that you have joined us speaks louder than words." As usual, John was very diplomatic and always encouraged his fellow workers.

When these seven Vol buddies were studying at Knoxville, at times they got frustrated when the experiments did not work out as they thought. As the most senior of them, John always came to rescue; he did not do the experiment, but encouraged them with words and suggested a different track of experimentation.

June was keen to know what was expected of her. "It looks like the physical requirement for our project has been set. It is our turn to staff the lab in the middle of nowhere. Is that right, John?"

"Yes, June."

Although the philanthropists and the scientists came from a different background and with different goals in their personal endeavors, they had a common denominator and conviction, which was "Peace without Bullets."

The meeting did not take long. Each member in that Faraday cage in the basement had expressed their thoughts that morning. And they departed just as they arrived, in a clandestine way, with the exception of Jack and Jerry. The two shook hands with Global Foundation senior staff, Mr. Erikson, Ms. Layug, and Mr. Kennedy, and mingled for a short time with the volunteers before leaving. The children of the volunteers were awed by the medals on their uniforms. Even after all these years, these two Vols had kept their figures, straight backs, shoulders high, no wrinkles, and no middle age bulges!

TERRORISM VS. PEACE

Before leaving the Global Foundation, John said to his friends, "Many thanks again for joining us. We will meet as a group, or just several of us, on and off during the next two to three years, whatever it takes. We shall work out the logistics of our experiments. How to divide the work to max out the efficiency in the shortest time, like Jack and Jerry have suggested. We will meet again soon as a group in the penthouse of Mr. Shum's hotel. You will receive encrypted emails. There is one point I must emphasize again—"

"Which is?" asked Ruth.

"It is very important for us to think seriously about our project. As I said before, it is a two-edged sword. Precisely, our work can be viewed as terroristic because there will be lives lost, albeit not amassing as those thousands if not millions of innocent people killed since the end of World War II. We have to sacrifice a small number of people and animals to demonstrate to the leaders of the world that we can target their lives if they don't quit making guns and wars. Here is what we have to discuss tomorrow. We will meet at the New Asia Hotel, which is one of hundreds owned by Mr. Shum of Hong Kong. We will use his penthouse suite with his private staff. Just walk in and you will be escorted, discreetly, to the penthouse.

"Guys," said John most soberly, "I cannot emphasize enough that our project can be considered terroristic, because we are going to blackmail the warmongers into destroying their war machines. This is your last chance to back out."

"John, can Harold and I come as a married couple?" June asked. "I just hate to be a lonesome dove. I'd like to have an escort once a while."

June was in her early fifties and the youngest of the Vols; she still turned the heads of men and women alike...

"You two make a beautiful couple," said Jerry with slight embarrassment.

"That is OK, Jerry," interjected Harold, "my late wife Rose knew about June and all of you. It was really unfortunate that she did not live long enough to see this project of ours. She would have been thrilled to have all of us together again and do this, what she would call crazy scientists' dreams."

"Come as you like," said John. "Ruth can come dressed as a homeless person, like the one in Knoxville, remember her? Come any time before ten. Oh, Jerry, I did not ask if Carol will be with you. She can come too if she wants. Or she can go shopping with Rita. Alex, our genius will come too. She is not only a genius, she is very unusual and mature for her age too. Her parents only know she is just one of the twenty students in a "Science for Youth" program set up by our firm. But she is the only genius among all the other smart kids."

Jerry replied, "Carol will come. She has a close friend in the city. I think they will do some sightseeing. They have not seen each other for a few years. By the way, Carol never bothers about knowing what I do in the army lab. She is involved with the church and teaches."

John nodded. "My wife Rita is the same way. But she has to help me do the PR, entertain clients, my boss, etc. She is indispensable to my position in the firm. As you know, there are a lot of dirty politics in industries like ours, probably more than in DC. My science is good; with the right politics, it is better. My firm is very happy that I am a board member of the Global Foundation. At times, they use that as PR too. The firm makes a sizable donation every year to the Foundation. In fact, we do have a number of corporations contributing to the Foundation."

With the specifics of their coming and going all worked out, they left clandestinely.

Each of them would receive encrypted emails in detail as their means of communication in the future.

DIVISION OF LABOR

In the lobby of New Asia Hotel was a waterfall with a fifty-foot cascade down a slanted glass plate thirty feet wide. The surface of the giant glass plate was rippled at random. When the water ran down the plate, it resembled real ripples in the creeks of the Great Smoky Mountains. To dramatize the effect of water, the architects designed a cave-like background with realistic stalactites as in the real natural caves. Colored lights changed at random intervals and with different intensity. In front of the waterfall were black-and-gold leather lounging sofas and chairs with colored-coordinated coffee tables; there were lamps and other decorative items to help guests relax while waiting for friends or having a drink.

Water was a symbol of fortune and good Feng Shui in the Chinese tradition. To Mr. Shum, these colors were gold and money. It was a big lobby with many uniformed personnel catering to the needs of their guests. On the left of the entrance was the registration desk with as many as ten clerks, young men and women of different ethnicities and speaking different languages as well. On the right of the entrance was an entrance to the ball room and other smaller conference rooms. Elevators were right behind the waterfall. One could not be more impressed by its décor which was grandiose but not gaudy.

When June and Harold entered through the massive glass turnstile front door, a bellhop in uniform came over and said, "Please follow me."

The three proceeded to a bank of elevators just right behind the waterfall. Like all other skyscrapers, elevators were divided into certain levels depending on which floors the guest rooms were located. There was one, however, without a specific floor notation. The bellhop used a key card to open the elevator door. The three of them got in. Within a minute or two, they reached the penthouse. As the door opened, Mr. Shum was there to greet them.

"Thanks, Joe, for bringing them up," said Mr. Shum to the bellhop. Then he turned to June and Harold. "Welcome. Please make yourself comfortable. The others will arrive momentarily."

Harold went to the window and looked out. He exclaimed, "Wow! What a view. Who was the architect who designed this building for you?"

"The architecture firm, E & E Design, built this hotel. They are twin sisters, Elizabeth and Esther, who graduated from Harvard and opened their own firm after working for a famous architect for a few years. After they built this building, we became friends, although I am about fifty years their senior—old enough to be their great grandfather. They call me Uncle Shum. They are now building two resort hotels for me, one in the Bahamas and one in Australia. They are much smaller and not high-rise. When we finish our project, we should all go there to relax a bit. For your information, it takes a crew of about a hundred to keep everything working in this hotel —that is excluding the hospitality staff."

The elevator door opened. Jerry stepped out with his wife Carol.

A few minutes later, John and Rita, along with fifteen-year-old Alex, exited the elevator.

Ruth, Jack, and Jim arrived individually a few minutes apart.

Mr. Shum again thanked the bellhop. "Joe, thanks again. I think we are all here. I will go down with you. By the way, Rita and Carol, if you want go shopping, just call the elevator. Joe will come up to take you down. When you return, regardless what time, Joe will again bring you up. If Joe is not there, his twin brother will. You can hardly tell them apart. They have been with me since they were born. I will leave you to your meeting and see you all later." With that said, Mr. Shum left them in the penthouse.

Oohs and aahs followed after Mr. Shum left and they took in their surroundings and the magnificent view across the city.

John addressed the group. "Mr. Shum was recruited by Mr. Erikson. I don't remember how, when or where. It had something to do with the Global Foundation building in New York. Mr. Shum was going to buy the whole block, raze the buildings and build this one there. Somehow during the negotiation, probably like us during our UNESCO day, Eric and Shum hit it off well. I am sure they talked about the world situation. Mr. Shum was not happy about the war etc. because his real estate and hospitality business have been affected in an adverse way, due to a decline in tourists, for example.

"Although Mr. Shum is nearly eighty, his outlook is of a fifty-year-old. He understands he might not live long enough to see this to fruition. He has written a will to give the Global Foundation fifty percent of his holdings. The rest of course, goes to his sons.

"By the way, there is a kitchen is over there, it is well stocked with all sorts of delicious dishes and drinks. Mr. Shum is a gourmet of sorts. He also likes to cook."

"A good friend to have," said Ruth.

"This is maybe the last time we all meet together for a period of time. After this, we will meet with or without me in twos or threes," said John. "We need to remain incognito, of course, as does our secret activity."

"Guys, may I make a suggestion?" asked Jack.

"Of course, Jack. You are the best spook here; and Jerry too," said John.

"There are seven of us," said Jack. "All of our bios, especially Jerry's and mine, are known and kept in probably more than one security agency, in addition to the military. National security is very sensitive about many of us scientists. On one hand, they need us. On the other, they fear defectors. So far as I know, they probably know we were all grads of UT. But our close relationship is known only to us. If all of us are together from time to time, security agencies will begin to get suspicious. There are scientific spooks, as per Harold, who keep tabs on all scientific work, not only in the military, but also biotech. Biotech could be developed into biological warfare or terrorism. So far, we are fine. China is very secretive with its progress and may actually be way ahead of us."

"There will be times we need to talk face to face. Not just via email or phone," said Jim.

"Yes," said Jack. "Here is what I propose. Two or three of us, no more, will meet when necessary—like at different conferences giving papers, talks, symposium, etc. We will sit and talk, just as with other scientists and colleagues. For example, June and I talk. Later and at a different time and different place, June talks to Ruth to transmit what June and I have discussed. This round-robin way will not raise suspicions that we are working together on some projects. However, there is one stumbling block, we do need to converse via cyber space to keep each other abreast. Face-to-face meetings don't give us sufficient time and information."

"There is a way to get around that," Jerry said. "But it will not be easy. We need to encrypt our conversation. And we cannot all use the same codes. For example, June and Ruth have one for themselves. Harold and I have another one, Jack and Jim another, and so on."

"Great idea, Jerry," said John. "The Global Foundation has just the right staff to help. In fact, that has been how all of us board members communicate. The board meeting is just a façade. And our government, probably that of many other countries too, knows who we are. But they don't know how we have been planning this for almost six years. We add members to the board from time to time. Some retire too. But our core, i.e. those you met on our Volunteer day, is sort of a secret club. Now you are part of us. But you will not meet us in the open. All the national security agencies know I am one of the members. Therefore I am the only conduit to the board."

"I admire their sincerity and vision. I didn't know they are spooks too," said Jim said a smile.

"Yes, Jim," continued John. "They are the most successful business people, industrialists, and financiers in the world. And they are very generous. For your information, since we met in the corridor of the United Nations during our UNESCO meeting, we have accumulated trillions of dollars. Of course not from me—I am well paid but not like these guys. The money is kept in their private accounts and in the accounts of their firms. Each of them, like us, has a firm commitment and conviction to try to replace wars with a new world order of peace. As we see the trend of the chaos in which we live now, the beginning of the end of humanity will be in less than a hundred years. With our kind of resources, we can buy the best, as the cliché goes, and we can accomplish our goal."

"That kind of budget is bigger than the NIH and NSF combined," said Harold.

"Right. That brings us to another task, that is, scientific personnel. We don't have enough time to train new recruits. Therefore we need to use our existing staff and associates. That means we need to send the best to the laboratory in Siberia for two to three years. I sort of figure that will be sufficient time to produce what we need to initiate the warning and create sufficient stock for several years. And we will need to keep a skeleton crew to develop new products as new threats may arise. By the time the methodology is ironed out, the production will be a routine matter."

Jerry asked, "John, you mean we need to pull our best assistants from their current jobs and send them to Siberia?"

Others echoed the same thought.

"Yes. They will be compensated enough for life, and will not need to seek further work if they so wish. However, as you may surmise, they too will be like us, super-secret. We will need to find legitimate excuses to extract them from their current positions without raising the suspicions of their coworkers or government concerns."

"It will not be easy. Many have families," said June.

"That requires personal skill," added Jack.

"Single people are a bit easier," suggested Ruth.

"Yes, it is not simple," agreed John.

"I have an idea that may work," said Jerry. "We will collect personal information on our candidates, more than what we have in our file—in great detail. We will hire some shrinks to help us to extract them. I like the word extraction!"

"Great idea, Jerry," said John. "That can be done. We can have top psychologists do that. They too will be well compensated and will be urged to keep the information to themselves. We don't need to tell them our task."

He added, "One of our board members, Ms. Paz Layug, will be an excellent coordinator for this particular task. We have accomplished a great deal this morning. Let's take a break."

John picked up the phone and called Joe.

Within thirty minutes, Joe and his twin brother Jack pushed two carts full of mouth-watering food into the penthouse.

"Let us know when you have finished eating," one of the twins said. "Call and we will come up to collect the dishes."

GENE EDITING AND NANOBOTS

After a great lunch and friendly conversation, the seven Vols went back to work.

John addressed the group. "When we get all our contacts' and associates' personal information, I will give it to Ms. Layug. She will use her resources and contacts world-wide to study them and make suggestions to us on how to talk to them into leaving their posts for a couple of years. She will personally interview them. She is very good at judging people. She is also very convincing, even in the most difficult circumstances and including persons with stubborn minds. I have seen her work magic. And we need them ASAP. Let us finalize our experimental protocols and goals. And how to coordinate, lab work as well as supplies. June, would you be our coordinator?"

"Sure."

"Hopefully we can wrap it up today," he continued. "Actually, we must. We will stay late if needed. We will. OK guys? We have agreed on the target genes in the Krebs cycle to slow down the metabolism. We will encapsulate them in nanobots. Delivery will be an airdrop as suggested by our young lady scientist, Alex."

"There are hundreds of nucleotides involved. Random targeting will not be effective," said June. "We will want to target genes that will let them 'die in good health.' That is our goal, right?"

"Right," said Ruth. "June, you are the enzyme lady, maybe you can narrow them down to a workable number."

John continued. "Jerry, you are the gene jockey. You can isolate them, sequence them to ascertain the characteristic or particular sequence that can be sub-targets for partial deactivation or suppression, i.e. slow them down but not completely deactivate them."

"OK."

"Harold," he continued, "you have been studying the fetal hemoglobin genes. Can they be modified, like adding or deleting a nucleotide or two, change their activation or expression?"

Harold nodded, replying, "Yes. But it's not perfect yet. We have been able to change a few nucleotides on one strand and not completely deactivate the pair, and, most interestingly, they can still reproduce and express just as normal hemoglobin genes will do. We used the technique called CRISPR-Cas-9."

"I have not seen the publication, Harold," said Jim, leaning forward with interest.

"No, we are about to draft one. However, with our task ahead, I will hold on to the data and procedures."

Jack added, "Jerry and Harold should be working together. John, did you say we will have different encrypted email that only two of us know, for just us, to maximize secrecy?"

"Yes, Jack. We have on our staff a genius who just turned twenty-one, Harrison. His mind is as mature as ours. He has been doing this for us for some four years. He is just like any twenty-one-year-old but has one very interesting characteristic—he can keep information to himself. In fact, he wants to use code names for us. He does not want to know who we are. Except he does know we want to have a new world order. He hates killing, even of an ant. I think he is Buddhist, not sure though. I will instruct him to provide us with codes. He will write programs for encrypted messages for us too."

"We have a computer geek and a biochemistry geek!" exclaimed Ruth.

"In addition to editing DNA, including mitochondria DNA, we need to consider degradable peptides. And don't forget RNA. In fact, RNA may be a better target than DNA because most RNAs, except ribosomal RNAs, are transient molecules, especially mRNA."

Jim spoke up. "CRISPR technology was developed for prokaryote DNA. China was the first to apply the technology to human embryos which were defective. There was an outcry on the ethical aspect. Many Nobel Laureates came out to object its use on humans, especially on germ cells. Maybe we can use CRISPR tech on RNA."

"Great idea, why not?" asked June.

"Let's identify the DNA sequences, both chromosomal and mitochondrial, and certain RNA too," said Harold. "Then we shall proceed to use CRISPR tech on both nucleic acids to synthesize what we need."

PHEROMONES AND NANOBOTS

"Delivery systems," said Jack. "I have been working on the microencapsulation of a mutant of an RNA virus, the Rouse Sarcoma Virus, in micro-robots. We are progressing slowly, you know, we only work 9 to 5 and a five-day week. My associate is very good, single too. He would like to work more but he is not allowed to because our labs are shut down at five and the security guys come in. So he spends his weekends in his basement making small mechanical robots and drones the size of a fly. Given the right environment, I would say one year top, he will accomplish what we need. The encapsulation of nucleotides is easier than an RNA virus."

"Jack, you got the job," said John.

June had a question: "John, your work on nano-robots, or nanobots, is impressive. Just one question, robots can carry things—can they be directed'to go to a particular target or targets?"

"They can be directed, or rather at this moment of our research, attracted to a particular target like a magnet. If we are to find a target, we need to study that target's characters in order to program the nanobots to be attracted to them."

Jack had a follow-up question too: "Jim, I remember you studied pheromones in insects and plants in Knoxville. Can we use the same approach for our tasks?"

"Yes, Jack, I did. And I have extended this pheromone phenomena from insects and plants to mammals. I have found similar substances in many mammals including human. I used to think that was why women wore perfume to attract men. Forgive my sexist joke—"

"Jim, we know you better," laughed June. "Please continue."

"Remember one of the guys in Knoxville, a big fellow, I forgot his name, M-- something? When we played softball in the evening, many of us used insect repellents. He did not. No mosquito would bite him. Why? It did not register in my mind until one day a big pharma sales rep stopped by to chat. He just mentioned that his firm's R&D was into something new, an anti-pheromone. That did register in my mind."

"So, mammals too have pheromone-like substances," said Jerry thoughtfully. "Different mammals have different pheromone like substances, like insects?"

"Yes."

"How long would it take to characterize or find a particularity in each different species and different individuals?" asked John.

"Not long, a week or less if a sample can be obtained," replied Jim. "There is one problem. It is species-specific. But within a population like us here, we might have different pheromones; let us just call it that due to the lack of an appropriate name at this moment."

"Meaning there might be several different ones in this room attracting different bugs?" Harold asked Jim.

"Yes or no; I cannot give you a definitive answer, not yet. Humans have not been inbred like wild animals. Therefore, we are more complicated, vis-a-vis probably having more varieties of pheromones."

"If we donate our sweat to you today, when can you tell us if we all are the same or different?" asked John in turn.

"Two weeks, top," said Jim.

"Damn, we already have a solid handle," said Jack.

"Once a marine, always a marine!" exclaimed June.

"Jim has got a job," John told the group. "When we find a target, Jim will be responsible for finding out what that target's character, attractants, etc. will be."

"No problem."

"If a program or a respondent molecule can be built into the nanobots, carrying our gene suppressors, we can readily direct our gene breakers at a target. It will be like what we are doing targeting different drugs at different cancer cells."

"The concept is the same," added June. "But the application is vastly different because we will be dealing with an open system, not a closed one like within a patient."

"Absolutely right," agreed John.

Harold had a thought: "Wait a minute. Do you remember what our young biochem geek suggested? Swarming, like bees?"

"That young woman is a genius, more than just a geek," said Ruth.

"So we should program the nanobots to swarm, or stick together, like bees, until they find the targets," concluded Jim.

John continued, "Let me summarize what we have discussed today. First we will identify targets we will sacrifice to serve as our warning to warring leaders as to what we can do. To do that, we need to find specific targets, and ascertain their pheromone characteristics. We will encapsulate the gene breakers into nanobots. Nanobots will be programed to specific targets to deliver the gene suppressors. Delivery will be airborne and the nanobots can swarm like bees around honey.

"Our nanobots and gene suppressors should be degradable or metabolized in the cytoplasm to eliminate detection. Therefore, we need to look for appropriate materials so the nanobots can enter into the cytoplasm that can do the job.

"I must emphasize that some animal and human lives will be sacrificed. Our project for world peace could be considered terrorism. In fact, we will blackmail and/or terrorize those leaders and nations who want war into giving up their warring ambitions and dismantle the factories of war machines. You can back out now if you wish. As I said, I trust all of us and I know with our concerted effort and the financial backing of the Global Foundation, we can succeed." John looked round at everyone. "Did I miss anything?"

"Yes," said Harold. "After we iron out the detailed synthetic process, we need to modify it for use on different species and individuals. And we will shut down Shelter 113. Future agents would have to be made in one of our labs. Maybe?"

"That will pose a problem since we do not work together. How do we put together all the parts?" asked Jerry.

At that moment, Alex and John's wife Rita came through the door with their shopping. They overheard what the Vols were discussing.

"I heard what you were discussing. Why don't you think along the lines of 3-D printing?" suggested Alex looking rather pleased with herself, before going into the other room with her packages.

A stunned silence spread across the room.

"Why didn't we think of that?" exclaimed John. "The Global Foundation certainly can afford to buy more than one machine and let Harrison have a new toy. We can probably have a room in the basement dedicated to that task. All Harrison needs are the experimental protocols and materials."

"Absolutely genius," added June. "Our minds are still back in our graduate training days. Good thing we have young mind like Alex."

"After we work out the biochemical procedure, we shall put Harrison to work writing a program to produce the agent with a 3-D printing machine. I am sure there are a couple of them that will work for us if we modify its design."

"If one of us tries to buy one, would that raise suspicions?" asked Ruth.

"It might. There is a way to get around it. We will ask Mr. Kennedy of the Global Foundation to discretely purchase a couple. It is almost 11 P.M. We have worked on this more than twelve hours."

John laughed. "It is like we were back in graduate days, except we don't need to sleep in the labs anymore! It has been fruitful," he concluded. "We can catch up on details with our encrypted emails. Remember, we all go back to work as usual. We need to persuade our institutions to let go of our associates for a couple of years. We can hire others to replace them. As soon as Ms. Layug and our psychologists 'extract' our associates, we will put them in one of Mr. Shum's hotels until we deliver them to Siberia."

"Before we leave," added Harold, "I think we have to coordinate the procurement of supplies, etc. June is the most organized one among us. Let June be our dorm mother again."

John nodded in agreement. "So, whatever we need, we will contact June via encrypted emails. And I will coordinate with the Global Foundation and Ms. Jankovic for transport and other details."

The seven Vol buddies had accomplished much and had worked out the details of experimental protocols. June would collect the data and coordinate the results once a week. They would proceed to the next phase using coded emails.

As they were about to leave, Jack turned to face all his friends and said, "Guys, there are two very important points that we must consider. We need to stay a bit longer, or meet again. These are practical issues and you may not like them. In the real world, they exist and we need to address them. One, how do we deal with someone, including a Global Foundation board member, if he or she decides to back out from the project and reveal what we have planned? Two, the CIA knows about everyone they need to in US, and abroad too. They know everyone's whereabouts, when he or she leaves and enters the country, and where they go. So extracting our associates will be difficult. How do we get them to our hidden laboratory in Siberia and back, when the task is done?"

There was no discussion nor any disagreement.

The facts did register in the minds of these Knoxville friends.

SHELTER 113 SHELTERING SCIENCE

The wind blew over the snow-covered landscape, kicking up snowflakes and forming a layer of thin ice with ripples on the surface as far as the eye could see. There were no other sounds or moving objects in the dead of winter in this most desolated region in Siberia. The rail tracks of the Trans-Siberian railroad were, however, free from piles of accumulated snow. Although there was only a twice-a-week run for passengers and freight between Moscow and Vladivostok, the tracks were kept in top condition by a snowplow. They were like two clean, parallel pencil lines on a piece of white canvas. Helicopters would fly over to make sure both freight trains and passenger trains were running smoothly and without delay. Even with such hazardous winters, the Trans-Siberian trains were the most efficient among all railroads in the world. There were plans to build a high-speed Meg Lev train like the one in Shanghai. The Maglev train between downtown Shanghai to Pudong airport was losing money. With such lengthy tracks, the maintenance would be beyond practicality. So Ms. Jankovic decided to just keep the diesels.

On a particular winter night, the dull rumbling of the train was heard louder and louder as it approached the dilapidated station called Shelter 113. The bright headlight cast an eerie shine on the white surface. The last car housed the workers and equipment. This car appeared to be like all other freight cars. Not so. Inside this car were the workers from Beijing and some equipment for the laboratories. Even with humans inside, their presence was undetectable by infrared red or heat sensors from outside, or by the spying eyes of any satellite.

The train slowed, and when the last car reached the track in front of the station, the train stopped and the car was uncoupled. While the train was picking up speed again, the track with the car was lowered fifty feet into the ground. After the car was pulled into the underground chamber, the track was raised again to fill the gap. The tracks again became continuous, clean pencil lines on a snow white canvas. During this operation, there was no light other than the headlight of the train which was more than half a mile or more away from the uncoupled car. The door to the underground chamber was closed to keep out the cold brought down with the car. As soon as the giant door was closed, LED lights were turned on, creating a soft, comfortable environment in the vast underground chamber. Ten Chinese workers from Beijing emerged with tools, gadgets and various building materials for the laboratory and residents. Mr. Chuen Lo, the crackpot engineer, and DJ, the big boss of these workers, came out. DJ would leave two days later on the return train to Moscow, then Beijing. Mr. Chuen Lo would stay behind to supervise the remodeling work.

With the blue print in a computer file designed by Ms. Lorraine in hand, they started work as soon as they had recovered from the long trip. Ms. Jankovic had placed six maintenance and catering personnel a few days ahead of the building staff. These six—three married couples—were Ms. Jankovic's relatives from Serbia. They were to stay in Shelter 113 to take care of daily needs, like cooking and cleaning, for the Chinese workers and the science associates until the end of the project, peace without wars.

The shelter, some 50,000 square feet, had simple furniture and a fully equipped kitchen, nothing luxurious but efficient. The whole underground chamber had originally been designed for top Russian Politburo members and their families, and it could house several hundred, with enough food and water for a month. Because of the emptiness it was not a difficult place to take care of. The workers and the maintenance crew did not know the end purpose of their job. They were told it was a top-secret, national-security matter, and they were to stay there for at least two years—very well paid. Periodically, they were taken to vacation spots other than in their countries of origin, for a short break, all expenses paid. They were told not to mention the underground shelter and what they were building in it. Since they were all trusted and loyal employees, the Global Foundation had faith in their silence.

In the meantime, Ms. Layug, working with psychologists hired by the Global Foundation, scrutinized the associates and assistants of the seven Vols. They took advantage of knowing their life history; therefore, there was no difficulty "extracting" them from their jobs, with the consent of their supervisors, the seven Vols. They were told that their work was sanctioned by the UN, the USA, China, and the EU. They were part of a secret, worldwide effort to combat a future epidemic. Instead of giving the jobs to big pharmaceuticals, they wanted to make the cost affordable to all the people in the world.

With one or two scientific associates from the laboratories of the seven Vols, plus one or two assistants together with a maintenance crew and building engineers, the total population in this big underground space came to no more than forty. There was plenty of room to move around. Mr. Chuen Lo was a seasoned jogger, so he built a jogging track around the periphery even though there were a few elevated, gentle bumps. Of course, there was a fully equipped gym; no swimming pool, however.

The Global Foundation, their employer unbeknown to them, did not ask them to sign a contract of non-disclosure or any contract related to their work. All the workers in this underground laboratory were told to keep the location secret, which was in the most desolated region of Siberia. They knew it was in Siberia, but they did not know the exact location. Their compensation was good enough for them to live out their remaining years in comfort, anywhere in the world, if they so wished.

The scientific staff was to report to their respective research directors once a week on their progress via emails or satellite phones, all encrypted without their knowledge. They knew their research directors were collaborators, but they did not know the purpose or the goal of their task; they would in time.

BEGIN TO MAKE PEACE

Two-and-a-half years from the day when the scientists went underground, the core of the trustees of the Global Foundation met in the sound- and electronic-proof Faraday cage in the basement of the Global Foundation building in Manhattan.

Mr. Erikson spoke first: "John, as I understand it, your scientist friends have accomplished an agent that can target a specific population or individuals in a mix, like picking them out from a crowd?"

"Yes, Mr. Erikson." John went on to describe the complicated scientific accomplishment in layperson's terms. "We select a certain population as sacrificial lambs. To do this, we studied a particular character found in that population. We synthesized a specific short DNA sequence that can suppress, but not destroy, the activities of certain genes. We target the mitochondria DNA. Mitochondria are structures in all cells in which there are series of chemical reactions called the Krebs cycle. These reactions in the Krebs cycle produce the daily energy need for all living processes. We synthesized a stretch of DNA with appropriate enzymes that can slow down these processes so that the individual will sort of slowly and gradually cease all functions for life because of the lack of energy. The effect will be a slowdown of their metabolism such that they will expire without any symptoms of illness. These short synthetic DNA nucleotides will be degraded in the cells back to their elemental forms—i.e. the four building blocks, in layperson's terms—upon expiration of the host organisms. These agents can reproduce once they enter the targeted individuals to yield sufficient descendants to enter all the cells in the body.

"We have developed a carrier system using very small robots, smaller than microscopic robots, at nano scale, we call them nanobots. These nanobots are also made from a component of cells called the cytoskeletons, protein molecules, we call them macromolecules. These nanobots will go directly to the targets because we program and build into them a natural chemical called anti-pheromones to react with the pheromones which naturally occur in living beings, plants, and animals including humans. All three basic components in these agents are natural biological components. Therefore, after they deliver the deadly blow, they disappear by mixing with the cytoplasm of the cells. No tests, as yet, can detect where and how they act."

Mr. Erikson asked, "John, have you identified any targets yet?"

"No. That will be decided today, here, if possible. Because it has been our goal, we should be the ones to decide the targets that can deliver the most severe warning to the warring leaders."

"We can pick out some animals first to see how the world reacts," said Mr. Kennedy.

"That is a good idea, good start," agreed Ms. Jankovic.

"If the world ignores the elimination of an animal population, then what?" asked Ms. Layug.

"That will be the next step; it may be more than one step," replied John.

"Humans? If we proceed to sacrifice humans, we would be considered borderline terrorists," said DJ of Beijing, alarmed.

"Yes and no," said Mr. Erikson. "Our aim is to have the warring leaders lay down their arms because so many innocent persons have been killed due to wars. "War for peace" is their slogan. We don't want that."

John agreed. "The number of sacrifices will be very small, much smaller, compared to the number killed daily with guns and bullets in the ongoing battles around the world."

"John, have you and the scientists talked about that?" asked Ms. Layug.

"Yes, we have. We can aim, so to speak, our agent to a particular group in a large mix population. Precisely, we have developed an agent that targets only the hyenas when all the animals are drinking from the same water hole in the Serengeti Sanctuary. No other animal will be affected; only the hyenas."

"What about humans?" Mr. Kennedy wanted to know.

"Yes and no, again. We have talked about using prisoners on death row, severely mentally ill patients, terrorists such as ISIS combatants, or a small population in the Amazon that have been inbred for years. The scientists would like feedback from the board."

"John, regarding what you have said about using humans, are the technicalities the same as with animals?" asked Mr. Shum.

"Probably not," interjected Dr. Rogers of Harvard.

"Dr. Rogers is correct," said John. "Getting samples from animals or humans will not differ much. But developing anti-pheromones will be more time consuming. In this room here we may have pheromones with particular characters not shared by others. That means we need to develop different anti-pheromone compounds. The same procedures but we need more time."

"If we used a small population that has been inbred for many generations it would make it simpler. Right, John?" Dr. Rogers, a scientist himself, had asked the right question.

"You are absolutely correct. Dr. Rogers."

"Have you discussed that?" asked Ms. Layug.

John nodded. "Yes, they need your input. I talked to Professor Alvarado before I came here. There are many small tribes in the Amazon unknown to the outside world. Professor Alvarado knows a few and she has contacts with poachers. You may ask, why poachers? Information from poachers is very important to the preservation of these isolated tribal people. She pays the poachers and provides them with GPSs to pinpoint the locations of the tribes. The Brazilian government does not do this, so they also have no knowledge of these tribes. We have identified several that we can readily sacrifice, if we decide that is necessary. The credit goes to Professor Alvarado."

"How many individuals in these tribes have you identified?" asked Ms. Layug.

Prof. Alvarado replied, "They are no more than 200; some just 100 or so. They have been living a very primitive life. We instructed our poachers when they find them, that they are to stay away, just take pictures, absolutely no contact. Poachers are very Amazon smart. They poach and kill animals. But they don't take the young and those in reproductive age. Unlike the big game hunters in Africa, these people don't consider the perpetuation of the species or care about their extinction. Amazon poachers are a particular population, smart, Amazon smart."

Ms. Layug continued her line of questioning. "For our project to create world peace and a new world order, we need to do something unethical such as killing humans and animals for the common good. Let us use the tribe with the smallest number of individuals. And, will they suffer?"

Ms. Layug was an animal lover. Her involvement must have been a dilemma and caused lot of lost sleep. In fact, that applied to all the board members of the Global Foundation. For those in the financial sector, like Mr. Shum, DJ, Mr. Erikson and Mr. Kennedy, the dilemma presented a lesser conflict in their heart. They were used to taking risks.

"By the way, Professor Alvarado, how did you get the samples of human tissue if poachers do not even get close enough to make contact?" asked Dr. Rogers.

"The poachers know the forest. They could tell where these people have been and look for signs like tree limbs that have been touched by the people. All we needed was a micro amount of DNA. So the poachers can collect minute tissue or, we can use DNA from finger prints such as left on our glasses here. It is not easy, it will take time. But they can do it."

Mr. Erikson looked around and asked: "Do we have a consensus to proceed? I have no problem with the hyenas. They are not an endangered species."

Ms. Layug had tears in her eyes. "My heart says no. But my mind says yes. For the good of millions of innocent people escaping from being killed with bullets, I agree we should proceed."

"Dr. Rogers, DJ, Mr. Shum, Mr. Kennedy—?" Mr. Erikson again looked around the table.

Noticeable nods from everyone was all that was needed to give John the OK. He took a deep breath. "Thank you. I shall work with my scientific friends to initiate our task. That is our first step. There may be more hurdles to jump over. Although we have taken all the necessary precautions. We know there is no perfect security. If leaks happen, we still have to depend on your contacts to keep us under cover. The Global Foundation must not be known as a villain. One more item—a very important one. After the scientific work, the people involved in Shelter 113 need to be able to continue the work elsewhere without associating with my friends. We will need another lab. We have talked about using 3-D printers as our future production laboratory."

"Has 3-D technology progressed to that degree for life sciences?" asked Ms. Jankovic.

"Yes," explained Dr. Rogers. "At Harvard we have several using biological materials as raw materials to produce simple biological samples. We are able to synthesize capsules, like empty nano-marbles, with amino acids, which are basic building blocks of proteins. With right computer programs, we can do much more."

"We need a room," said John.

"We probably can build a room here," replied Mr. Kennedy. "There is no problem buying one or more 3-D printers. We can have Harrison write computer programs according to your protocols. Would that work, John?"

"Yes. I will come frequently to work with Harrison and check the product out myself."

Mr. Erikson would have a difficult job presenting this difficult task to the other members who never were involved in the day-to-day matters and activities of the Global Foundation. A couple of them were high officials in their respective governments. They remained anonymous, only known to Mr. Erikson. They never asked how their contributions were to be used. They did however understand that other board members had the vision and ambition to make the world a better place, a new world order. They also knew the Foundation wanted to convince leaders of many nations not to start wars. They however did not know the means. When they heard about the means for the goal involving humans as sacrificial lambs, they might have the same dilemma as all other members of the board as well as the scientists.

Before the board members left the room, John said: "There are two problems which we have to address. They are practical and unavoidable possibilities suggested by our scientists in the military, Jack and Jerry."

All the members of the board sat down again.

"John, please proceed. As we said, we will finish when we finish," said Mr. Erikson.

"First: How do we deal with someone, including all of us here and the scientists, who decide to withdraw from the project—worst scenario, reveal our plan?! How do we prevent that from happening? How can we find out before he or she decides to withdraw? How do we ensure trust among us?

"Second: Jack and Jerry told us that the CIA knows everything about every individual in the USA—when they quit their job and why, when they leave the country, where they go and why. Of course, not everyone, just persons of interest. The CIA has the means to see the telltale signs of suspicious individuals, especially scientists and their associates. The super computer constantly checks and cross checks all those like us. As you know, since 9/11, charity organizations like ours have been under scrutiny; scientists too because of their potential to defect or to be bought by enemies, to go rogue, to do harm to the world."

With that said, John sat down, and reached for the coffee.

There was silence for a few minutes. Some helped themselves to coffee or tea.

Ms. Reyes broke the silence. "John, this is real and we do live in a real world. After all, we are all human and humans make mistakes."

Mr. Kennedy picked up the thread of thought: "I believe we, i.e. us here, can address the second problem. It will be illegal. And if the CIA finds out, we are all doomed. Professor Alvarado, Ms. Jankovic and Mr. Sonnovovitch may—I said may—not have to face the consequences. I cast doubt because our project is a worldwide geopolitical cause. I am sure the UN and major powers like the USA, China, Russia, and the EU will try to find out who is behind it. In the end, all of us, and all of our good deeds will come to zero."

"How can we, or what role can—?" Dr. Rogers was sort of speaking to himself.

The room lapsed into silence again. Obviously everyone was in deep thought, confused thought maybe.

"I believe we can help with the second problem concerning the CIA. I need consensus however," offered Mr. Erickson.

"What is on your mind, Mr. Erikson?" John asked.

"We can hack the CIA. Specifically, we can keep the files of the associates of our scientists from being in the category of potentially suspicious individuals because of their work. I believe Harrison can do it without much difficulty. Recently, a thirteen-year-old hacked into US Navy personal files including those of several admirals."

"We still need to fabricate stories as to why the associates are leaving their posts. Co-workers may ask. We need appropriate answers," said Professor Alvarado.

"Yes," agreed Mr. Sonnovovitch. "We need to coordinate with your friends, John. Timing is important too."

"That can be done. How about the first problem, ensuring trust?" asked John.

Dr. Roger stroked his chin and looked thoughtful. "John, I think we—that is, you and I and the Vols—can develop some means by which to ascertain who may be thinking of quitting. I need to think a bit more about it."

Ms. Reyes looked decisive. "First, let us ask Harrison about hacking into the CIA. Can it be done and if so, without being traceable back to us? The CIA does have good computer experts. I can ask him now and let him give us the answer tomorrow. We can canvas our consensus via our encrypted emails."

John looked relieved at the positive response. "I will convey our discussions to my scientist friends to see if there is a possibility of addressing the first problem. Of course, we will have to fabricate different stories for each individual associate leaving his or her post."

"If it were not for Dr. Jack and Dr. Jerry, I would never think about these realistic probabilities," said Mr. Shum.

"In Russia we have much closer scrutiny of government employees, like the CIA. I think China does too. DJ, right?" said Mr. Sonnovovitch.

"Yes, we have a closer watch means too," agreed DJ. "But government orders are always followed. Dissension is not tolerated. Therefore, problems brought about by Jack and Jerry do not usually happen in China, but not absolutely."

Mr. Erikson brought the meeting to a close: "Ladies and gentlemen, we have achieved the scientific aspect of our project. The problems brought about by Jack and Jerry are real, a human problem.

Each of us could be the candidate bringing down our dream of a new world order. We have to be realistic. John, would you and Dr. Rogers look into the technical means to ascertain who may have the tendency to withdraw and reveal our project? I will consult with our members to address the CIA angle. Is this agreeable to all?"

All the members agreed to proceed. With no more discussion and no solid resolutions either, they left the Faraday cage in the basement of the Global Foundation building.

THE FIRST WARNING

After the soul-searching meeting in the basement of the Global Foundation building, all the board members left with heavy hearts.

Mr. Erikson called the computer geek, Harrison, to his office in the presence of Ms. Layug and Mr. Kennedy.

Mr. Kennedy explained, "Harrison, this is the first time I will tell you the real goal of our Foundation. The goal is to change the world, institute a new world order. We, with our vast resources, think we can convince the leaders of warring nations to lay down their arms. There have been too many innocent people getting killed because the leaders want war disguised as a means for peace. They think war is good for the country. We think otherwise."

"All these charity works?" queried Harrison.

Mr. Erikson replied, "All these charity works are the façade. We have accumulated a lot of money, due to the generosity of many, and contacted many top scientists to work on our goal. Remember we asked you to program the encrypted emails of several scientists so they could discuss their findings without knowing by whatever or whomever?"

"Yes, I remember. I did not know, and did not ask why."

"And we asked you to write a computer program for the two 3-D printers in the new basement room?"

"Yes. I did, although I did not know the science behind them. By the way, did the machines make the correct products?"

"Yes. Harrison. Dr. John and Dr. Roger both have completed a standard 'wet' assay. They were perfect. And we have applied them to real animals and people. You will know in just a few minutes."

"I'm glad."

Mr. Erikson proceeded to summarize the history of the Global Foundation, how the Foundation had been able to present itself to the public and government as nothing but a charity organization. He also told Harrison how they recruited—via John, whom Harrison knew—several top scientists to develop an agent that could cause the victims "to die in good health."

"I have trouble with this method of using sacrificial lambs. But I think there are no other more convincing words to a bunch of blood-sucking warmongers," said Harrison.

Mr. Kennedy shuffled his papers. "Harrison, can you send something to all major TV and radio stations in the world without revealing that it was sent out by us? Same with hacking into the CIA. I mean that the message and hacking cannot be traced to us?"

"Yes, I can just go to a computer café and use their computers. However, these cafés have cameras and they record who comes and who goes and when. Once they have my face, they can easily find me here."

"So, using computers in a café is out," determined Mr. Erikson.

"We cannot use computers in this building. I think, but I am not sure, national security agencies monitor traffic in and out of organizations like ours, big or small." Harrison paused, closed his eyes for a short time, then continued: "My very good friend and I share an untraceable computer, at least we think so. I may have to use that. We spent a lot of time programing it without a back door. Most computer security people come in through the back door rather than the front door to keep perpetrators from knowing. We use it for fun stuff, nothing serious."

"Well, can we use it?" asked Ms. Layug.

Ms. Paz Layug treated Harrison like her own son. Harrison also liked her. They would frequently go out for lunch or dinner. Once in a while, Paz would go to Harrison's apartment to clean up, straighten up things, and make sure Harrison had sufficient healthy food in the refrigerator. Geeks like Harrison often forgot to eat and sleep when they were on to something. Sometimes Harrison forgot to come to work. However, work here, until now, was child's play for him. And Mr. Erikson never bothered with it because he knew Harrison well. So did all the staff in the Global Foundation.

"Yes, but no guarantee," said Harrison. "Like Confucius said, 'In the company of three, one can always be your teacher.' There must be someone out there who may be able to trace the messages back to our computer."

"What if you destroy your computer after sending out the messages?" suggested Ms. Layug.

"That is probably the only way—throw it in the East River. That will be a real waste!" said Harrison.

Ms. Layug was the one who really understood Harrison. He could relate ideas and concepts seemingly far apart that appeared to be unrelated for many ordinary people.

Mr. Kennedy said, "Harrison, as I told you, we have unlimited resources. A mere computer can be replaced. We can do that."

Harrison sought to explain: "Mr. Kennedy, it is not just one computer. It took three computers with super computer capability. My friend and I did it for fun. That means we have to throw all of them into the East River because each one has some information buried deep in its memory. Some smart guys can retrieve them. I think government agencies have some very smart people too. TV stations have nothing. We can cut in anytime during the broadcast without them knowing who we are or how we do it, or prevent us from doing it. But we don't do that. Just to make sure you know."

"If TV stations cannot trace back to you, does that mean you can send out our warnings to world leaders without being detected by national security agencies?" asked Mr. Kennedy again.

"No, Mr. Kennedy. Government guys will just go to the stations using their programs to try to track us."

"How fast or how soon can they trace back to you, if they can?" followed on Mr. Erikson.

"A couple of days. May be three if they are just as good as we are."

"If we send out one warning, wait a few days, or a week, then send out the next. Can they trace back within that time?" persisted Mr. Erikson.

"Yes, if they are good. We have to assume they are good."

Mr. Erikson looked pensive. "We can replace your computers easily. But the work and time you, and whatever your friend installed in the computers, cannot be. That means you have to start over again after you dump the computers into the East River. Am I correct?"

"Yes."

"You and your friends' previous and existing works will also be sacrificed," concluded Mr. Erikson.

"Yes, we will do it because we dislike war and killing all those innocent people," Harrison emphasized his belief. "What about the statement or announcement?"

Mr. Erikson replied, "Yes. We have written the following for you to post on all TV and radio stations. Oh, yes. Can we post them in twenty languages simultaneously? I think there are programs for simultaneous translation into many languages?"

"Yes. The computer can send them out without the stations knowing their origin—all known languages too."

Mr. Erikson handed a sheet of paper to Harrison. "Here it is. I have written it out in English. I will however read it to you to see if any editing is needed:

'To all nations: Three weeks ago, a large number of hyenas in the Serengeti died while all kinds of animals were congregating at a watering hole. No other animals there were affected. Two weeks later, every member in a small tribe in the Amazon also died. In both cases, the experts of worldwide organizations, including the CDC of the US, the WHO, and Mossad could not find any cause or causes. We, an organization of peace for humanity, have shown you world

leaders that we are able to target and eliminate a specific population even in mixed hordes, like the Serengeti. And we can also do the same in human populations. We can even target one individual among hundreds. Our purpose is to convince you to stop killing innocent people because of your continuous war activities. This is our first serious warning. Our next target will be officials of nations at war who do not comply. We want you to call back your soldiers and tell them to lay down their arms; destroy your killing machines and close all your factories making them.'"

"We will send it out to see what response we get," said Harrison.

THE BALANCE OF POWER

Ever since the disastrous 9/11 terrorist attack that killed thousands of people and brought down the Twin Towers in New York City, there was no single day without the death of innocent people, including many children. The most volatile region was the Middle East. President Nixon had in fact predicted in one of his books that this region would be the most troubled one to come.

The wars and the casualties of wars claimed millions of lives. It did not seem even to reach the beginning of an end. One blessing was that none of these battles involved nuclear weapons. All the political leaders and people in the world realized the immediate and long term destructive effects of nuclear weapons. It was a blessing that humanity would not vanish anytime soon.

Nevertheless, leaders of every country considered that tanks, missiles, fighter planes and weapons of mass destruction were beneficial for their economies. Innocent casualties were just part of the investment for domination whatever the value may be. Unbelievably they claimed it was all done for the sake of peace...

The economy in many third world countries, especially those in Africa, had improved to the level that they could not be called third-world countries anymore; and the longevity of their people lengthened thanks to an immense development fund from China and the EU. But people in Africa, just like in other places in the world, wanted more. In the dark ages, they fought for food based on pseudo-religious beliefs. With the advent of a higher living standard, one would think that the tribal culture and wars in Africa would have disappeared. Not so—the tribal culture persisted. Nowadays, it was supplemented with gun powder.

The United States was still the strongest military and economic power in the world. Its commitment to NATO countries had dragged it into war with Russia, albeit indirectly, which risked developing into a direct confrontation. At the same time, the US was involved in the chaotic religious wars in the Middle East—Israel, Iraq, Iran, Saudi Arabia, Syria, and ISIS, as well as many terrorist groups. The world had changed but not for the good. Religion and war had again become a synonymous ideology.

In the Oval Room in Washington D.C., the Secretary of State addressed the President of the United States. "Mr. President, with our support of Israel and Saudi Arabia, there should be a balance of power in the Middle East."

"True," the President replied. "But that may be the root of the trouble, dating back to the nineteenth century and earlier."

The President was a political historian. He had been a professor of history at Yale before he was drafted by a third party to run for the presidency. The general populace had been fed up for years with the old guards in both Democrat and Republican parties. Their traditional, old-fashioned dealing with both domestic and foreign policies was based on military strength. The economy took a second-class, back seat. The election of an academician into the White House represented a breath of fresh air and a new ideology.

Did it work for the benefit of the USA or for world peace?

"We have been involved in the Middle East conflicts for many years, too many, and with no end in sight," the President continued. "Remember at the end of the eighteenth century, France was fighting Austria over Italy. The reason was the economy and commerce. France wanted a piece of the reward from trading with China via the Silk Road."

"With the precept of a balance of power, when you came into the Oval Office, Mr. President, maybe we could accomplish what Bismarck did with the unification of the eastern and western Prussian tribes," said the Secretary of State.

"Reunify the Middle-Eastern countries like the Ottoman Empire before Great Britain and France divided them arbitrarily? As at the end of World War I?"

"We have been giving them billions of dollars in aid for development, in the belief that a balance of power would end the wars. Dr. Henry Kissinger was the most vocal proponent of a balance of power."

A reluctant expression on his face, the President shook his head lightly. "But we did not achieve that balance. Thousands have been killed and we, frankly, have played a role in it."

"Maybe we should have given them military aid, like training their soldiers and arming them with military hardware, tanks, and missiles."

"The Muslims, Shiites, and Sunnies have been at each other for thousands of years. Minor religious cults like ISIS had been in hiding for a long time. Now, with a general economic improvement, they can afford to buy guns. In addition, the Christian population has increased to the level that they represent a formidable political component there."

"They all have nuclear warfare capability. I hope they don't suddenly decide to bomb each other." The Secretary of Defense looked worried.

The President looked doubtful. "I don't think they will. If one crazy leader wants to, it will be the beginning of World War III—possibly the beginning of the destruction of humanity!"

"But Mr. President, Turkey is at the crossroads of the Middle East and Eastern Europe, and will not remain neutral when that happens. There is too much at stake for Turkey, especially its economy. The Turks may just want to return to the glory days of the Ottoman Empire."

ASIA THEATER

In Asia, previously poor countries like Myanmar, Vietnam, Thailand, and the Philippines were no longer poor. With their increase of economic power, each had enlarged its military force. Countries in the South China Sea region, including India and those above, claimed many islands as their territories. Battles that had been fought with words in the past were now being fought with bullets. The only losses were for the innocent islanders whose previously relaxed lifestyle was disrupted, and at worst destroyed. Tourist trade was near zero. While the governments of these previously poor nations had become richer, the native islanders had not. They not only had become poorer but also had become endangered species!

Guns and bullets in South Asia echoed those in the desert of the Middle East. Although China and India had not formally declared war, battles along their borders were putting residents in the war zones of both countries in jeopardy. They had no place to go. Refugees flooded the mountain roads. Indian and Chinese refugees mingled and tried to help each other, while their governments' soldiers aimed their guns at each other.

While gun battles were raging in the Himalayan foothills, diplomats from China and India were in conference on the third floor of the United Nations building in New York City.

"Mr. Chan, yesterday over a hundred students were killed by your missiles that landed in a middle school," said Ambassador Singh of India.

"Yes. Mr. Ambassador," replied Mr. Chan. "Missiles do misfire at times. Your largest air force base is in the proximity of the school. In fact, they overlap and share the football field. Is that right?"

"Yes. It is. But that is not an excuse for your mistake."

"Mr. Ambassador, you and I know that there will be collateral damages of war. All of us try to prevent that from happening to civilians. It is our responsibility to protect them and to make sure they are not in harm's way." Mr. Chan was, however, a representative of China, not an ambassador to the UN. He offered no apology. The meeting between the Chinese and Indian diplomats ended without a handshake. They walked out without even looking at each other. Their staff did the same.

China and Japan were engaged in battles over fishing rights. Fishing boats were armed with short-range, sea-to-sea missiles. They tried to destroy as many of each other's catches as possible. Sometimes the fishing boats were so close, they could shout at each other.

Historically, Japan's ambition was territorial gain. Japan had no natural resources but the sea around it. That was the reason for the Japanese invasion of China at the beginning of the twentieth century. During the World War II there was a Holocaust in Germany and the Nanking Massacre in China. While Germany apologized to the Jews, Japan attempted to hide the fact. The undeclared war between China and Japan therefore contained the hidden context of revenge for the Japanese invasion. Japan could not fathom the fact that China had overpassed it in both economy and military might.

No other nations, including China, had a naval force equal to that of the United States. The mighty 7th Fleet was pulled back from the South China Sea to the west coast to protect against possible attacks from Russia and Japan. Therefore, it offered a free zone for the Chinese navy.

China had just a few aircraft carriers while the US had twenty. China realized that there could be no match of large battle ships for offensive purposes; it therefore concentrated on the development of fast mobile fleets, with many small submarines capable of cruising at forty-five knots. Submerging time was short, however, while US nuclear submarines could stay submerged for months at a time. The strategy of the Chinese navy was to use the aircraft carriers as refueling stations for the small submarines. They only carried a few small fighter-bombers. The coastline was well defended by fast destroyers and an unknown number of small subs.

With overwhelming naval strength in the Pacific, the Indian Ocean, and the South China Sea, China blockaded crude oil tankers to Japan. Japan now relied on nuclear power plants, some fifty in an area no bigger than California. Most of the nuclear power plants were in the east coastal region of Japan—many of them on isolated islands close to the main islands. In peace time these locations were advantageous in case of accidents. However, they were vulnerable to attacks from the sea. Taking advantage of this vulnerability, small Chinese submarines would periodically torpedo several of them to cripple their generating capacity. In addition, containment of the leakage was difficult, rendering a radioactive dead zone around the plants.

Japan could no longer exercise its sophisticated military power because her neighbors were just as strong. With the unification of North Korea and South Korea, Korea had become an eyesore for Japan. For hundreds of years, Japan had suppressed Korea, and there were no warm feelings between these two countries. No Japanese fishing fleet dared to come close to the seven-mile off shore over which Korea had declared sovereignty. With the South Korean's economic power and North Korea's military machines, they had unified and fortified their defense against a possible Japanese invasion. Although the unified Korea had no naval force like the US or China, they had the power to defend their long coastline. Korea had remained free of war for many years and its people were the only population living in peace.

RESPONSES TO THE MYSTERIOUS DEATHS

The selected death of hyenas among many animals in the Serengeti Sanctuary was ignored by the world, except those in the management of wildlife in Africa. The death of an entire tribe in the Amazon was treated as a natural anomaly in the Amazon. Since no cause for the deaths had been found, people around the world soon forgot about it since the media considered the events unsensational for their readers—there was no financial gain. Therefore, there were no further reports on that subject. Warring leaders of the world ignored the warning from the Global Foundation. Some governments even considered the warnings from the Global Foundation as coming from a crackpot, or even crazy kids sending out a naïve message—maybe a practical joke?

However there were concerns, serious concerns, among animal management organizations and scientists at a few institutions. Among them was the US Center for Disease Control, where a small group of scientists, headed by a Nobel Laureate Dr. Young, was assigned the task of finding out the cause of the deaths in the Amazon. When the Global Foundation's warning came out, they immediately went to the director of the CDC, Caleb Morrison.

"Mr. Morrison, although we have not found the cause, we should pay attention to this weird message from whoever sent it out. We may want to find out whoever is responsible," said Dr. Young.

The director nodded. "Dr. Young, it did not escape my mind when the message appeared after these deaths of animals and humans. I think it is serious enough to raise a red flag with Washington. I will be there tomorrow for a routine annual report to the Senate committee on health. I shall see what they think. I am sure some of them may laugh it off too. Are there any clues from your group?"

"No sir, not a clue. Not yet at least. We still have many samples to analyze. Not finding any clues means whatever technology these people used has potential—an advanced technology unknown to us at this moment."

"What kind of potential? A bioterrorist group we have yet to know?"

"It is a possibility."

Across the Atlantic, the European Counterterrorism Center, Europol, was concerned—not as much by what the statement said, rather by how every TV station on earth simultaneously received the statement, and in the language spoken by that region. It was considered a cyberattack, or a practical joke, rather than a warning or a threat to their leaders' war games.

Missiles were still crossing the sky in the Middle East. They literally ignored the message from the Global Foundation.

YOU MAY BE NEXT

Two weeks after the first warning announcement from the Global Foundation, there was still no serious thought by the warring nations to reduce their war games. The thousands of innocent people killed were still considered collateral damage, just the norm in conflicts and battles between nations.

When the Brazilian government revealed the death of the small primitive tribe in the Amazon, and released the pictures taken by the poachers, some leaders, then—and only then—started to take the events and announcement seriously.

At the same time, another announcement came out with a one sentence message, broadcast to multiple communication outlets and in as many languages as the first one.

"Within one week, similar incidents to the deaths of the hyenas and people in Amazon will happen if you continue to ignore our first warning."

It was the season of large migrations of animals in Africa. Among them were herds of jackals. They preyed on the weak and young buffalos. In the midst of the migration, hundreds of jackals suddenly died like the hyenas. No other animals were affected. The buffalos did not seem to notice.

Still the warring nations ignored the warnings.

In the Middle East, ISIS was gaining an upper hand against Saudi Arabia. They openly revealed who their leaders and lieutenants were. They were at the outskirts of Riyadh. It appeared that ISIS would take Riyadh within days.

At nightfall, twenty advancing ISIS commandos suddenly died in their tents while having dinner. The manner of their death was identical to those in the Amazon. They just died as they were; some even had smiles on their faces.

When that news reached the world, alarms, real alarms, went off.

A short communication in multiple languages again appeared on all TV stations:

"Stop fighting, pull back your armies, and close the armament factories within one week. If not, major officials in your countries will die like those in the Amazon and the ISIS commandos."

Security agencies of every country frantically attempted to find out the origin of these messages. Some warring nations blamed each other. Countries with superior technology, especially biotechnology, were blamed for the cruel acts. Countries in Africa, the Middle East, and South America formed a coalition within a week, casting blame on countries in the northern hemisphere who wished to dominate the world with their superior biotechnology. The southern hemisphere considered the messages as blackmail from the north in order to force the southern hemisphere into surrendering all their rich resources—just as the British, Spanish, and Portuguese had done in the sixteenth century with gunpowder.

SITUATION ROOM IN THE WHITE HOUSE

The President of the United States summoned his cabinet members and selected officials government to meet in the Situation Room in the basement of the White House, including the Vice President of the US; Secretaries of State, Defense and Treasury; National Security Adviser; Senate and House leaders; and the CDC director as well as Dr. Young.

The President entered and started to address his audience before he had even sat down. "Ladies and gentlemen, thank you for coming at such short notice. I am sure you know why. I am taking these messages and the death of animals and humans very seriously."

"Yes, Mr. President," was murmured around the table.

"First, Caleb, please brief us," he said, turning to the Director of the CDC.

The director cleared his throat before replying: "I have triple-teamed our top biologists and medical doctors to examine samples for all incidents. We still have no more clues than we had with the Amazon and African incidents. Zero! We are dealing with a group of very unusual, very talented scientists with advanced biotechnology unknown to us at this moment."

"Alfred," the President asked the director of National Security Agency. "Have you come close to finding the source or sources of the messages?"

The Director of NSA looked at his notes before answering: "Mr. President, I must admit that we did not pay much attention to the first lengthy one when it reached all the major TV stations worldwide. When the second and third came out, we began to put our best tracing programmers to work. The messages were short, but we were able to trace them to a supercomputer in the state of New York. We have not narrowed it down to a city yet."

"Could the lack of clues mean we may be dealing with not one, but a group of scientists in secret collaboration?" asked the President.

"Yes, Mr. President," said Dr. Young. "It would be difficult for this work to be done by one laboratory. Our counterparts in Israel, China and Russia have considered a rogue nation, individual, or a group of individuals who have developed the technology in secret."

"We have contacted directors of research in these countries to monitor the works of their staff," added CDC director Morrison. "We have not come up with any suspicious individuals or groups of individuals."

The President turned to the Secretary of Defense. "If we assumed the work was done in one laboratory—I am sure we know the nature of all the biotech labs and pharmaceutical firms—and assuming work has been done with a moving lab, (which may not be likely), can our satellites detect unusual activities?"

"Yes, Mr. President, if it existed."

"What if it was underground?"

"That is possible, sir."

"With regard to the messages—although they were sent from somewhere in the state of New York, could the messages be from nationals of other nations routing through New York to confuse us on its origin? Could this be possible?" asked the President.

"Yes, sir," said the National Security Adviser.

"Should we pull back our troops from Ukraine?" the Chairman of the Joint Chiefs of Staff asked the room.

"We have scheduled aid to several Middle East countries. Should we hold back on it?" added the Secretary of State.

The President signaled for coffee. He let his cabinet and staffs discuss the options.

"I think the threat is real," the President said with a barely detectable shake of his head. "I don't want any of us, including me, to die like the Amazonians or the hyenas. Obviously, these people have more personal information on the victims than just resumes."

As an academician, this US president thought differently about world politics than his predecessors. He had also read the famous book, "War Strategy," by the Chinese war strategist Sun Tze.

One of Sun Tze's strategies was *"A step backward could be two steps forward."*

His mind made up, he addressed the group: "We will pull back our troops in Ukraine a few miles from the Russian border. Hold back on the aid to the Middle East. Let us wait. There will be a UN Security Council emergency meeting on this weird but deadly event. Dr. Young, please attend that meeting with our representatives. Good day, ladies and gentlemen." That was the signal for ending the meeting in the Situation Room in the basement of 1600 Pennsylvania Avenue, Washington, D.C.

BEIJING, CHINA

All over the world, cabinets of presidents and premiers were in conference as in Washington, D.C. Members of the Chinese Politburo were also in conference in Dong Nan Hai next to the Imperial Palace, now a museum. Tiananmen Square was closed to the public. Since every household in China had more than one TV set, just like citizens in the United States, few Chinese were unaware something extremely important had happened in the world, not just in China.

Premier KS Li first turned to Dr. Wen of the Chinese Academy of Sciences. "Dr. Wen, is there any progress on the origin of the strange communication?" asked the Premier.

"Yes, Premier Li," the Director replied. "We have traced the first one to New York City. The other two appeared to come from the same origin. We're not sure because the messages were short. The sender or senders were very smart. We could not find similarities in our repertoire of cyber-signatures. They seem to be from some amateur teenager but I don't think they were."

"I think the messages are serious enough for us to heed the warnings. Like Sun Tze said, one step backward could be two steps forward," said Premier Li thoughtfully.

"Premier Li, I believe we should pull our soldiers back from Tibet," suggested General Ho. "Two miles back from the border. Surface half of our subs in the Pacific, east of Japan. Have them sail back to Tianjin."

"Do we have other options?" asked Premier Li.

"We probably should give all the workers in our armament factories a vacation," added General Ho.

"Does that mean we accept defeat?" challenged Ambassador Lee who had just returned from the UN.

"No," replied Dr. Wen, "We are not at war with a particular national group or nation. This organization has obviously developed a biotechnology so sophisticated it is years ahead of our own."

"Dr. Wen, could this technology have a base in genetic technology?" Premier Li asked.

"Yes, Premier Li. Definitely. There is no poison that could have such particular and unusual effects."

"Do we have samples and have we done all necessary analyses?"

"Yes, we have the same result as the US CDC and the Israeli counter-terrorism group, which is part of Mossad. That is, no known technology that can effect death in such a manner. A nursing mother died with a smile on her face!" Dr. Wen said, and turned to the director of the newly created division of biosecurity within the Liberation Army of the People's Republic of China. "Dr. Leung, what do you think?" he asked.

"I agree," said Dr. Leung. "In fact, we have been in contact with our counter parts in Israel, Germany and France. We think this 'poison,' for lack of a specific term at this moment, must affect the genes or expressions of certain genes. The Germans think this group has created an Ebola virus mutant. The French scientists think it might be a benign pox virus which could be degraded by naturally existing enzymes. Therefore, this agent would escape detection with currently-known analytical methods."

"Let us do what we just decided. Then we will wait to see what the US, Russia, and the EU are going to do," said Premier Li confidently.

MIDDLE EAST

The United States, China, Korea, Russia and other countries in South Asia took the warnings from the Global Foundation seriously. They pulled back their troops but did not close the factories that made weapons, except in China.

Countries in the Middle East, including Israel, ignored the warnings.

The Republic of Palestine and Israel were still at war. Since Palestine became a republic, accepted by the UN but not by Israel, its economy had improved some tenfold. They hired mercenaries to train their fighters with modern weapons. Suicide terrorists with bombs strapped onto their bodies were no longer a threat to the Israelis. They were replaced with missiles capable of hitting intended targets. Several Israel army camps and hospitals were hit, together with civilians that were in close proximity.

Palestine missiles targeted at Israel were almost a weekly event, and the Israelis were doing the same. In fact, Israel was considered the worst country for human rights by the UN because Israeli missiles had destroyed several hospitals with the death of hundreds of children. Only the US gave a dissenting vote in the Security Council.

One morning, a week after the last short message from Harrison and friend, ten commandos of Palestine fighters, and an equal number of Israel soldiers failed to wake up for breakfast. They all died in the same manner as those in the Amazon village and the animals in Africa.

They died in good health!

Because of these forewarned deaths, every country that had engaged in war with casualties of their civilians ceased to fight. Even the armament factories in the United States, Germany, Japan, and France were deactivated. Workers were furloughed.

UNITED NATIONS SECURITY COUNCIL

The Security Council of the United Nations immediately held an emergency conference. Premiers and presidents were busy calling each other to keep each other informed (a rare occasion since the establishment of the UN in 1956). Each country began to exchange data on their examination of the tissue samples and circumstances surrounding the events.

"Thank you for attending this emergency meeting." The chairman, Dr. Wang from China, addressed the fifteen members of the Security Council. Dr. Wang was a technocrat with a PhD degree in computer technology from the University of California at Berkeley. He was better qualified than a politician in this sort of matter. Ambassador Lee, China's ambassador to the UN from China, had been recalled to Beijing.

With no more introductory remarks, Dr. Wang continued: "There are four essential points that we should consider in our discussion. Any suggestions will be welcome.

1. Origin or origins of the threatening announcements. If we find out from where or from whom, we can deal with them.
2. Method or methods of inducing death to particular groups or individuals without affecting those in the same area or close by.
3. Who are these perpetrators, obviously including scientists, who developed these deadly methods?
4. Location or locations of the laboratories where the work was done.

While I have the floor, I will summarize what we in China have found, albeit very little.

Point 1 – We have a rough idea that the first warning came from the state of New York, probably New York City. The other two may be from somewhere else. There is no common cyber-signature on all three announcements. Our analyses showed that the diction and the nature of the linguistics mean the messages appear to be written by

Americans. However, that is not realistic thinking because most of computer experts in the world were trained in America.

Point 2 – We have not come up with anything solid. We think it is based on genetic technology.

Point 3 – There must have a very well-funded scientific endeavor.

Point 4 – We have no solid clues that point to any of above.

Ladies and gentlemen, please add to what we have. Maybe we can come up with some answers by pooling our resources."

A member of the US delegation spoke first: "I am Dr. Young of the US CDC in Atlanta. At the CDC we agree with Dr. Wang that the agent or agents were formulated based on genetic technology, i.e. genes or a group of genes have to affect in concert to bring about such strange death. Whoever designed the agent has to know the genetic background of the dead individuals and the animals. Getting the genetic background of animals is easy. The perpetrators must have vast resources, both financial and human, to know the genes of all these dead individuals. The soldiers in Israel and Palestine were not twins or inbred like the people in the Amazon village."

Dr. Young had been awarded the Nobel Prize five years earlier for his study of and its subsequent influence on molecular therapy. He had been recruited from Vancouver to join the CDC in Atlanta and was a highly respected scientist.

The next response came from the Russian ambassador to the United Nations, who was listening to Dr. Young's words interpreted in real time through his headset. Instead of speaking in Russian, he addressed the room in English, with a touch of hostility in his voice. "With all due respect to you, Dr. Young, and to your American colleagues, we have detected that both the language and the means may have a tinge of Americanism."

"No offense taken," said the American delegate diplomatically. "We also think that the US and China would have such resources and scientific capability."

The Russian ambassador continued, "On the location of the work, it could be in a laboratory in a hidden location. Or, it is a collaboration of several laboratories at different locations."

The attractive French ambassador spoke next: "We first thought this agent or agents might be mutants of Ebola virus or polio virus. But the symptoms, or more precisely lack of symptoms, make us cast doubt on our earlier theory."

"Are there possible alternatives?" asked Dr. Wang.

"Yes, but they could be farfetched," continued the French ambassador. "Neither a virus or mutant. It may be a short nucleotide or a peptide like the cause of Mad Cow disease. If it was in fact a peptide like that for Mad Cow disease, the animals affected in Africa would sort of wobble a bit before they died. And the Mad Cow peptides cannot be digested by intracellular enzymes. We should be able to detect its presence in the cell and tissues. Does that work for humans? We do not have an answer."

"Dr. Rosenberg, your assessment?" Dr. Wang looked over to the Israeli desk. Dr. Rosenberg from Israel was in his thirties, thick glasses with bushy hair. He spoke with his head slightly tilted to the right, with a squeaky voice. "We too have traced the first announcement to the state of New York, probably New York City, maybe the second one from Africa, Uganda, and the third from China. However, the only tentative affirmation is New York State. Whoever sent them out can route the messages via thousands of sites worldwide. We too thought they were by Americans because of the way they were written in English. However, as Dr. Wang mentioned, the majority of computer experts were trained in America. But that is just a guess, for now."

"Our technical experts have run thousands of traces in our Chinese webs, we could not find any clues at all, even though all the messages were in Chinese on Chinese networks," replied Dr. Wang.

Next to speak was the UK delegate: "We too started with our own network and checked all the public internet cafés with the thought that he, she, or they may have used public computers that are not easy to trace. Even if we could trace them to a particular computer, we would have no idea who the renter or renters may be. Not every internet café here in England has monitors."

"How about infectious agent or agents, for lack of a better description of them?" asked Dr. Wang asked the UK delegate.

"Our colleagues at the Royal Academy of Science think it is more likely a nucleotide rather than a peptide. The reason is that nucleotides can bind to introns and exons that can be deactivated without destroying the DNA double helix. If that is the case, of course we don't know yet, the effect may not be on one gene but multiple genes. We think genes-control metabolism would be the likely targets."

"Dr. Young?" Dr. Wang looked over at the US desk.

"We too think it is more likely to be nucleotides rather than peptides. But we cannot rule that out anything yet."

Dr. Wang asked another exploratory question: "These terrorists must have abundant resources, both personnel and monetary. I don't think work like this can be done by one individual. It must be an organization unknown to us. Ladies and gentlemen, are there any organizations or institutes in your country, or anywhere in the world, that may have that capability?"

"Other than America, China would be the only country who can do it. No offense, gentlemen," said the Russian delegate.

"We cannot rule out any possibility or probability," said Dr. Wang diplomatically.

The French delegate disagreed: "I think it is more likely an international conspiracy. With the ease of communication most successful industries or individuals are in the realm of global enterprises. I don't think we can say they come from one country."

"I agree," said Dr. Rosenberg.

Chairman Wang closed the meeting: "We have exchanged what we know about this dangerous act for humanity. We need to continue to pool our resources, exchange information, everything we can." With that said all the delegates filed out of the room except Dr. Wang, Dr. Young, and the American delegates.

One of the American delegates asked, "Dr. Wang, is that true that your army at the border with India has pulled back?"

"Yes, two miles. Our satellites revealed that you too have pulled back from the Russian border at Ukraine."

There was a reason for Dr. Wang's answer, or statement rather. Dr. Wang was not only a technocrat; he was also a trusted right hand of Premier Li of the PRC. China wanted the American to know that China could monitor every movement of American troops in the world. It was a subtle warning to the Americans of the Chinese technological superiority or equality.

"Maybe America should consider shutting down their armament factories as well," suggested Dr. Wang.

"We are willing to take the risk, for now at least."

The delegates from China and America shook hands.

SENATOR NGOI

There was rarely a full house in Congress except when the President gave the State of the Union address in January every year. Today, however, the Senate was almost full. Sitting in the center was Senator Ngoi (D) from California.

As usual, the Senate and House of Representatives were always involved in all popular issues, both significant and trivial matters. These particular events of animal deaths in Africa and the villagers in the Amazon had just become an emergency in the Senate. And, as usual, useful or usable results from hearings were rare. Members of Congress had to earn their living and show their constituents that they were concerned about the welfare of their constituents, as well as doing good for the nation and the world. This hearing had drawn much attention not only in the US but also across the world because the bio-agent(s) had the potential to affect human destiny.

Ten years ago Senator Ngoi was in general dentistry in a small town in California. Because of his disposition, kindness and caring, his practice was booming after just a few years of practice. He was well known around town, not only for his practice, but for his community services; for example, he donated his time to migrant workers and the poor who had no health insurance. One day, a freak accident caused the loss of dexterity in the fingers of his left hand, his dominant hand. That ended his dentistry practice. While there was much disappointment from his patients, this dental group with three dentists continued to be a great service to the public.

Rather than sitting idle, Dr. Ngoi sought advice from his tennis club members although he no longer was able to play tennis at the A level because he had to play with his right hand, not his dominant hand. One of the members at the tennis club had been a member of Congress. With the urging of this retired Senator, Victor, Dr. Ngoi was persuaded to run for office.

"Ngoi, I think you will make a good addition to the Senate. We desperately need someone with compassion and medical knowledge. How about it?" asked Victor.

"Victor, I have no experience in politics, and never took a course in political science or anything close to it in college. But I don't want to sit idle the rest of my life," replied Dr. Ngoi.

"Ngoi, you don't need experience in politics. It is just a game, a verbal game of empty promises. There are just a few sincere ones. Not enough."

"I am surprised you said that."

"Ngoi, we have known each other since high school days in San Francisco. I served three terms. I tried to be a good public servant. That was an illusion. So I retired and am now a gentleman farmer. You know the rest."

"You know I will keep what you just said to me in confidence and off the court."

"I know. The public is fed up with politicians. A fresh face will win. Especially in California where the majority is non-white. And none of our members in the Senate have experience with Hispanics and other minorities like the Chinese and Vietnamese. The last two groups will be a formidable political force if they have representatives in the State Legislature and DC. You know as well as I do, almost 90% of the policies have been ignoring benefits for the Hispanics and Asians who fortunately have been a huge resource as they work hard, and they are rising above the economic level of the whites."

"Running for office needs money and experience. Especially me. I have never run for any office, not even in high school or college," said Dr. Ngoi doubtfully.

"I will be your campaign manager and coach," said Victor persuasively. "I have some seed money; my dear wife left me a bundle. My kids are grown and both of them are successful in their own endeavors. In fact, Christine retired at fifty. You know about her and her brother Huber. Not only do they not need me, they have enough and some to spare. Huber just bought a Ferrari, his tenth sports car. He has a fulltime mechanic keeping them all in excellent condition."

He added, "I just talked to them last week about my idea of your running for the Senate. They were so excited. You know, you are their favorite. They are willing to help, both financially and with legwork. With their bank accounts, we probably will not need contributions from anyone else. I think they have enough to put you in the Senate. You are a good speaker and have a great disposition. Here is a chance to show your talent in addition to drilling teeth!"

"Victor, I have never had a twinge of desire to run for public office. I do agree with you that there are not many good men and women in Congress, especially in the last ten years. Our current President seems to be doing a good job. I like him."

"Yes or no?"

Dr. Ngoi took a sip of his decaffeinated iced coffee and thought for a moment.

"You talked me into it," he said.

Victor slapped his friend on the back and said excitedly, "First, we will expose you to the public. You don't need local promotion because everyone older than ten here knows you. In fact, we can probably draft many volunteers to help. I will form a committee with many locally-known people, my son and daughter, and the PR person who put me in the Senate. Remember, I had no experience then. I do now. What I want you to do now is to go to the gym, shed a few pounds, increase your stamina, just be healthy and in good shape. The worst thing for a hopeful candidate is fat! You are fine. You just need to increase your stamina. That is a start. I will do my part."

"Just tell me what to do. Someone has to write a script for me to follow."

Victor used his cellphone to make several calls. "Paul, I need you to be on my committee to put Dr. Ngoi, you know him, in the Senate in DC—Yes, Dr. Ngoi, the dentist—he cannot practice anymore because he lost the use of his fingers on his left hand, his dominant hand—yes, we old kooks can try—thanks. See you at the club next Sunday, 10 A.M.

"Tony, I need you to be on my committee to put Dr. Ngoi in the Senate in DC—yes, he was your kids' dentist—he had to retire because he broke the fingers on his dominant hand— no, he can't drill your teeth any more—can you meet me and others next Sunday , 10 AM? Great.

"Kirby, Victor here, how are you? We need to draft you—to put Dr. Ngoi in the Senate —yes, in D.C., not Sacramento—Can you meet us next Sunday here at the club? Good, see you then— around 10 A.M.

"Andy—how is the family? Good to know he will be at Harvard—How about Rita? — Harvard too—We need you to work with us old tennis buddies—put Dr. Ngoi in the Senate—yes, D.C., not Sacramento—Dr. Ngoi is hurt, actually he broke his fingers on his left hand, his dominant hand—no, no more practice of dentistry—10 A.M. on Sunday—see you then.

"Jenny—yes, me Victor—my kids are great. I think they have more money than God—we need your organizational skill. The reason I'm calling is we want to put Dr. Ngoi in the Senate—no, not Sacramento—he lost the use of his fingers—a freak accident—10 A.M., next Sunday, at the club—Andy, Tony, Paul, Kirby are in—we may need more—we are the core—yes—see you Sunday.

"Christine, I have contacted Andy, Tony, Paul and Kirby to form a core for the election committee for Dr. Ngoi. We will meet at the club Sunday at 10. Can you come?—Good. Would you contact your brother too? Oh, yes, we will need a lot of money—thanks, see you.

"Sharon, how is business? Good to know. Can you take time off from your travel agency to help Dr. Ngoi? —Yes, the dentist for all our kids and adults—we want to put him in the Senate—D.C, not Sacramento—we need you for the travel plans—yes, can you get a bus and other travel plans for Senator Ngoi? 10 A.M. next Sunday—Great, at the tennis club, thanks, see you."

Dr. Ngoi was impressed. "Thank you, Victor. I can let my associates do the routine work. Wow, Victor, I am going into politics!"

Two weeks into May, a big bus was to be seen with "Dr. Ngoi for US Senate" emblazoned in large print on the sides. At the rear of the bus was a retractable platform on which Dr. Ngoi would make his many campaign speeches, like the old-time whistle stops on the railroad tracks.

In November of the same year, freshman Senator Ngoi moved into the Senate building in Washington, D.C.

Many colleagues in the Senate had difficulty pronouncing Ngoi, just like the citizens in California. In time, however, the word Ngoi took root (name recognition at the maximum). Some even had fun saying it. And that only added to the popularity of Dr. Ngoi. Whatever statements or speeches he made in the Senate had actually carried more weight, therefore, more political power.

UNITED STATES SENATE HEARING

Scientific members of the UN-led scientific investigation committee, supported by the USA, China, Israel, and the EU had been able to isolate themselves from the media. These countries had given strict orders to the media to stay away from the scientists so they could devote their time to finding a solution, and to identifying possible scientists or groups who were capable of creating such a bioweapon. The urgency to find the culprits was not a political matter. It concerned the possible destruction of humanity. The second reason was actually not obvious to the general public. Each of the major powers wanted to be the first to have that bioweapon. The third reason was to prevent a rogue nation or group from getting hold of it by buying it or even kidnapping scientists.

Numerous essays, opinions, editorials, and critiques filled headlines and monitors in every corner of the world. Many institutions of higher learning had in fact structured special courses solely devoted to this subject since the deaths in the African wildlife sanctuary, a whole small tribe in the Amazons, soldiers in the Middle East and civil servants in the US. In addition, celebrities who were dog and cat owners had lost their pets right at pet shows. This particular episode had elicited interest, special and covert, in big pharms and nations with vast financial and scientific resources.

Would the development of this deadly bioweapon follow a similar track as nuclear weapons?

With national security in mind, the US Senate sprang into action as soon as the last warning was sent out to the world by Harrison. A special committee was formed in a few days and hearings were started in less than a week, a record time for any action in the Senate. The Senate committee first assigned computer experts to trace the source of the warnings, hitting a dead end just like all security agencies in the world. At the same time, the Senate Committees on National Security and Health began to work together to find a solution because the cause of death involved both. The

Senate did as the Senate does best—a special hearing was held with members from both sides of the aisle.

The presidents of the three biggest pharmaceutical firms—one from the US, one from Sweden, and one from Singapore—were invited to the hearing proceedings. Directors of the CDC, the NIH, and the US Academy of Sciences made up the six initial expert witnesses. The first phase was to hear the science and health aspects of the bioweapon.

The senate committee was bi-partisan, two Republican and two Democrats with Senator Ngoi (D) in the chair. He started the meeting: "Ladies and gentlemen, thank you for consenting to be expert witnesses on such short notice. As we know, this sudden death of humans and animals, pets included, in the recent months, were phrased by an individual or group as warnings or means to achieve world peace, a new world order.

To that end, there have been no battles or killings for more than six months. Does that mean whoever they are have achieved their aim or goal? This is the strongest weapon ever developed in the history of civilization. It can wipe out a whole population such as those in the Amazon. And it can target selected individuals, like the soldiers in Israel and Palestine and the civil servants in our own government. If this bioweapon falls into the wrong hands, we don't have a thread of optimism for peace. And, we don't know who these perpetrators are, or if it is the act of a particular rogue nation who did it, with a context of peace, as they said. Did they? Is their intent a Samaritan act, or the prelude to some unethical, immoral blackmail?

"Ladies and gentlemen, the purpose of this hearing is to cast light into who or what organization had the capability to formulate such a deadly weapon. Secondly, how long would it take to develop this particular methodology? Thirdly, can an antidote be developed? None of us in the Senate has expertise in molecular biology or molecular therapeutic methodology. That is precisely the reason we have invited our honorable guests to cast light on this matter. To help us solve the riddle, so to speak, before it gets out of hand."

For an opening speech of any hearing, this was a short one. Ordinarily, the chair would take some twenty minutes or longer. The chair may ask other members to make short statements before questioning the witnesses. The whole morning sessions might have been occupied with the politicians' favorite pastime—to hear themselves talk, to show their constituents that they were working for them.

"Dr. Ebert. Thank you for coming." Senator Ngoi looked over to a gentleman, slightly bald, about mid-seventies. Dr. Ebert moved up to a chair at the center in front of some ten news media journalists, some of them facing the senate panel and others facing the witness.

"Senator Blume from Massachusetts, would you start, please," said Senator Ngoi.

"Thank you, Chair Ngoi. Dr. Ebert, you have been elected recently the president of the US Academy of Sciences. Prior to that, you were Director of our National Science Foundation. Am I correct?"

"Yes. Senator."

"In your distinguished career in science all your life, have you ever imagined some group or groups would develop germs, or if they are germs, a better word would be bioweapon, as our President called this agent? I assume this agent is of biological origin, since none of our esteemed scientists here and abroad have detected unusual physical or chemical elements in the victims, both human and animal. Oh yes, Dr. Ebert, you have distinguished yourself in molecular biology. Correct?"

"You are right. I am a molecular biologist specialized in the embryonic system, Senator Blume. It had to be biomaterials."

"You must have reviewed numerous resumes of scientists, as well as scientific reports. Did any of them ever give you a hint of this kind of scientific idea—maybe bioterrorism is a better word? I don't mean the authors themselves. I meant someone might have mentioned this idea."

"Once in a while, some may have mentioned bio-warfare. But I don't recall reading anything close to what we have experienced. Germ warfare is not new."

"Dr. Ebert, do you think this work could be done by one deviant individual?"

"No, Senator. It has to be the work of several, or even many laboratories."

"Dr. Ebcrt, clarify for us if I am wrong. I was reading not too long ago that Chinese scientists have used this technique called —*[the Senator looked at his notes]*—CRISPR-Cas 9 to modify DNA in human embryos. It was American scientists who were credited for its invention. Do you think this CRISPR technique could be a candidate?"

"Yes, Senator, it is possible."

"If the DNA was changed to be fatal, can we detect the changes?"

"Yes. But we have not detected any changes in thousands of samples with currently available techniques."

"Chair Ngoi, I have no more questions for Dr. Ebert at this time. Thank you."

"Thank you, Senator Blume. Dr. Ebert, would you please stay? Senator Willis from Mississippi, please take the floor." Senator Ngoi looked over to his right.

"Thank you, Chair Ngoi," said Senator Willis in his booming voice. There was probably no need for a loudspeaker when he addressed a nearly-full house in a room as large as a basketball court.

"Dr. Ebert. I flunked biology in high school. I didn't dare to take biology in college. *[There were chuckles from the audience.]* Therefore no science beyond high school for me. I went into law and learned a little logic. *[Senator Willis was flipping through his notes]*.

So far, we have not been successful in detecting any changes in the DNA of the victims. How about other changes?"

"Senator Willis. I studied biology because it is straight forward, there is no logic involved," said Dr. Ebert. A few chuckles were heard in the audience.

Dr. Ebert had been an expert witness numerous times facing the Senate and Congress since he became, what was called, a biopolitician. The definition of biopolitics was vain yet at the same time specific and practical. Politicians played word games and made correlations for the benefit of their constituents, and for their own re-election. Since scientists have difficulty conveying their findings and benefits to the general populace, many laypersons would not understand the significance, let alone its future implications for human welfare. Dr. Ebert not only was able to convey scientific significance to laypersons, especially politicians, he had rescued many worthy programs and saved several institutions from closing due to funding. Because of his research in immunology, organ transplants had been successful in more than 80% of the cases. From straight bench science, Dr. Ebert used his oratory talent to keep and expand scientific research by convincing governments, i.e. politicians not to deemphasize basic scientific research. Life has been much better in the last two centuries because of basic research.

"OK, Dr. Ebert," Senator Willis said with a smile. Senator Willis too had a good sense of humor. With his booming voice, no one could miss his jokes in the Senate cafeteria.

"Dr. Ebert, to continue down the same path as Senator Blume, CPI—you know the technique—can this technique work on cell components other than DNA?"

"Yes, Senator. It certainly is possible, like RNA."

Before he asked the next question, Senator Willis turned to his aides behind him and whispered something. One of his aides gave him a sheet of paper from which he phrased his next question.

"This note I have here says the dogma of molecular biology is DNA to RNA to Protein. DNA is the master molecule that directs RNA to make proteins. My amateurish interpretation. Am I wrong?"

"No, Senator, you are not wrong."

"There are probably thousands of chemical and biological, or even physical, processes based on this dogma in our cells and tissues. Would it be like finding a needle in a haystack if this needle is the key process for killing all these innocent people and animals? Or, inflicting injuries—no, breaking the reactions of multiple chemical and biological processes, in and out of the cells, that are needed to create this deadly bioweapon—from molecular therapy to molecular bioweapons; inflicting on human welfare and humanity etc.? Our tasks here are twofold, more than that, multifold. Who and where were these bioterrorist materials made and to whom were they delivered for peace, as it was phrased? Perhaps there is a covert ideology of not peace but of power. "

Senator Willis was known to ramble, mixing words and ideas in many hearings. As a Southern gentleman he made full use of his demeanor to his advantage. He was able to disarm witnesses who may want to purposely hide facts. Of course, this morning's session was nothing like that. But that did not change Senator Willis' manner of speech.

"Yes sir. To create this bioweapon agent or agents is not a simple biological or chemical reaction. It most likely involved several laboratories here and abroad."

"Dr. Ebert, why 'here and abroad'? Or why not here or abroad?"

"I actually meant the procedures involved were complicated, not straightforward like making a sharp knife."

"Yes. I understand. Dr. Ebert. Are you aware of the UN-lead team to unravel the mystery?"

"Yes. I am not part of the team. However, our President has asked a few of us to be informed regarding the details of their findings or hypotheses."

"Are they on the right track?"

"Yes, they are. These scientists are the best among the best. I know a couple of them,"

"When they find a solution, any one of these scientists can begin to produce that bioweapon back home."

"It is certainly possible."

"Thank you, Dr. Ebert. Mr. Chair, I have no more questions at this time." Senator Willis had concluded his questioning.

Senator Willis was a shrewd investigator. No one in the audience, including the panel, had any idea of the implications in this simple question. He had placed the committee members in the UN-led, super-summit science committee on the "persons of interest" list.

Senator Ngoi continued, "Thank you, Senator Willis and Dr. Ebert. Senator Ballinger from the great state of Oklahoma. Please take the floor." He looked over to where Senator Ballinger sat. Dr. Ebert left the witness table and returned to his seat.

"Thank you, Mr. Ngoi. I have a few short questions for the distinguished pharmaceutical industrialists," said Senator Ballinger. "Gentlemen. What I had in mind may not be relevant to our hearing or in finding the perpetrators or groups who have developed such a powerful bioweapon. This is a general question for all. The question is whether there is an application for health, i.e. in the medicinal aspect. Mr. Poon, please."

Mr. Poon was a CEO of a big pharma in Singapore. His company had produced several effective drugs for the common cold, lotions to prevent insect bites, remedies for arthritis, and other drugs for non-fatal illnesses prevalent in the tropical regions.

"Thank you, Senator," testified Mr. Poon. "Our major emphasis on drug development has been on the relief of non-fatal illness such as the common cold, insect bites etc. In the past two years, we have started to explore the role of genes in the differential sensitivities, reactions to allergy and immunological reactions. To that end, research into possible changes in DNA with the CRISPR technique for the development of preventive drugs is a new venture for us."

"Thank you. Mr. Poon," said Senator Ballinger. "Mr. Sorenson, thank you for coming all the way from Sweden to help us to unravel this mysterious and deadly weapon. I am sure all of us here, and in every corner of the world, want to find out who is behind this. Your firm has been a leader in health care through genetic engineering and molecular therapy. Your firm's noble notion is to cure genetic diseases. This group appears to want to terminate life, with the pretext of peace, also used the approach at the genetic level. Do you have similar perceptions as many scientists and governments around the world?"

Mr. Sorenson nodded. "Yes, Senator. We certainly do. We are far from knowing. Theoretically, given time, is it possible to do the same."

Senator Ballinger continued, "Thank you, Mr. Sorenson. Dr. Jones *[that is John, one of the seven Vol friends]*, you are VP of R&D of AZ Pharm, the biggest pharmaceutical company in the world. Other than many marvelous drugs developed by your company, I learned that your company also formulates delivery systems for drugs produced by other companies worldwide. The global interaction of business and technology in the context of mutual benefits has been my interest even before I joined my distinguished colleagues here. In fact, I was with your firm in the mail room in my high school days."

After these lengthy remarks, Senator Ballinger then asked, "This bioweapon agent would need some kind of carrier such as capsules, regardless if it is liquid or solid. Would my assumption and thinking be on the right track?"

John nodded. "Yes. You are correct, Senator. One important part of our R&D is carrier systems using nano-encapsulation with biodegradable materials."

"Ingenious. Can you tell us what that may be?"

"Senator, this would be proprietary information which I am not allowed to divulge in public. I must ask you to direct your inquiries to our CEO, Ms. Kung," John said.

"Sorry I asked. I should know better," said Senator Ballinger with a smile. He added, "Chair Ngoi, I have no more questions for these gentlemen."

"Ladies and gentlemen, it is almost lunch time. Let us take a break and resume at 2 P.M. By the way, I would be glad to invite you and your associates to our cafeteria. However I cannot arrange a private room. If you wish, these young men and women wearing blue blazers will show you the way." With that said, Senator Ngoi left with his aides trailing behind, taking all sorts of documents or notes with them.

At 2 P.M. sharp, the senators, witnesses and the audience filed back into the Senate hearing.

"Senator Ballinger, I understand you still have a few questions. Please take the floor again." Senator Ngoi said.

"Thank you Senator Ngoi. Mr. Sorenson, thank you again for travelling such a long way to come. As I understand, your firm was the first to treat Tay-Sachs disease and sickle-cell anemia with genetic technology. The treatment has been over fifty percent successful. Am I correct?"

"Thank you Senator. The treatment has actually been nearly seventy-five percent successful," answered Mr. Sorenson.

"Will it soon be a hundred percent?"

"No Senator. No treatment is a hundred percent successful. But that is our aim in the medical field."

"Is the CRISPR technic part of the processes? I don't want your proprietary information. CRISPR technology appears to be a powerful tech in genetic engineering. And it is evident that whoever developed this bioweapon may have used CRISPR as part of their protocols. CRISPR tech has been in the public domain for twenty years or more. Given time and resources, can your firm, or any pharma with the right scientists, make such a weapon?" Senator Ballinger had the habit of showing off his scientific knowledge.

Senator Ballinger had a degree in nursing. He was the president of the National Nursing Association before he stepped into big politics. He had support not only from nursing but also from other paramedical professions because he was able to help them gain a rightful professional status and fair compensation for their services.

"Senator, I can give you a very strong negative answer." Mr. Sorenson was obviously annoyed. "We have no plan or even a minute notion of working on such a bioweapon. Our endeavor, and I am sure the same of all of our professions, is to heal, not to kill."

"No, no. Mr. Sorenson, I did not mean that. I was referring to the technical know-how. We have briefings from the UN-led super-summit committee. It appears to me that whoever did this is pretty far ahead of our current genetic knowledge. And pharmaceutical industries are very much in the biotech of the future." Senator Ballinger rambled on. "In order to find out who has been behind this deadly act, public and private sectors need to cooperate. Just one more question. Mr. Sorenson. In your assessment, what would be the minimum time needed to produce such a bioweapon?"

"It took us ten years of research to find the solution of Tay-Sachs and sickle-cell anemia. That, of course, was just us in Sweden. I would guess with an international effort, this bioweapon or a similar one can be achieved in three to five years."

"Thank you, Mr. Sorenson. Chair Ngoi, I have no more questions."

Josh, an aide to Senator Ngoi, handed him a yellow folder. Senator Ngoi opened the folder and pulled out three pictures. One of them was a mother nursing a baby with a smile on her face. That was the picture taken by the poachers in the Amazon. The second one was a soldier who seemed to be having a good dream. He was an Israeli commando. The third one was a deputy assistant in the US Treasury.

Senator Ngoi propped these pictures up facing the audience and looked grave.

"Ladies and gentlemen, you may remember seeing these pictures recently, like within the last twelve months. These are victims of the deadly bioweapon. They were the sacrificial lambs. Yes, there have been no deaths of innocent people in a year or so since all warring parties pulled back their troops and took their hands off the triggers. The world has been peaceful except for isolated incidents that still exist. I think it will continue. Like chemical reactions, there is no 100% complete reaction. Our goal is to find out who produced this bioweapon and how it was done. Our goal is to gather information and ideas from you on how the best way, if any for now, to make the best from this unusual method of achieving peace. And most importantly, we want to have some idea of how to prevent such deadly technology form falling into the wrong hands. There will be a subcommittee to address the security issues."

Senator Ngoi continued looking over to where Dr. Ebert sat. "Please stay where you are, Dr. Ebert. You were a director of our National Science Foundation that oversees creative research in science as well as education. Now, you are the president of National Academy of Sciences. That is absolutely the most distinguished accomplishment for any scientist. Can you tell us—if you go back a year or two, with research proposals and current scientific activities here and abroad serving as historical background—could you have predicted what has happened?"

"Chair Ngoi, thank you for your compliments. Molecular biology has been the subject for the largest number of research proposals in the past five years. Gene editing with CRISPR-Cas9 and Cpf1 has been the major technique proposed among many. From my recollection, all these proposals have one thing in common— to cure genetic diseases and create modified food-based animals and plants. I don't think I ever read into them, or could I have predicted what has happened."

"What is Cpf1?"

"That is another gene-editing technique similar to CRISPR, much easier but not as versatile."

"I think this question was asked but please elaborate. The question is, are there individual molecular biologists or groups of biologists capable of synthesizing this deadly bioweapon here in the US or with collaboration worldwide?"

Dr. Ebert thought for a moment. "I think there are many talented scientists here and abroad who can do this. It does not need international collaboration. Advanced technological nations like China, France and others would have enough talent, but not single individuals, to carry it out."

"With what kind of timeline?"

"Two to three years, may be more. That includes not just the agent or agents, it would include carrier systems as well."

"Please give me lesson one. What would be the starting point or material? I assume it would start with DNA."

"You are right, Senator, it has to start with DNA."

"Dr. Ebert, how does one get hold of DNA? Can you obtain my DNA from my finger print?" Senator Ngoi lifted up the bottle water, took a sip.

"Yes, Senator. More than that. Agencies like the FBI, CIA and other security agencies have stocks of DNA samples of employees and many common citizens. Many of them have been sequenced and stored in various computers. For example, in my lab, we have the DNA of many species of experimental animals and plants, in addition to the real biological materials. We have elucidated their sequences and stored them in our computers. Depending on the experiments, we can just lift them out, the whole gene or a portion of the total molecule for specific experiments."

"In other words, if some smart hackers wanted them, he or she can just hack in the computers of the FBI and CIA to get the DNA of whoever?"

"Yes, Sir. It has been done."

"We should not have such collections for whatever security reasons, in other words."

"Senator Ngoi, that is not for me to comment. It was decided some time ago by the Senate in this room."

Senator Ngoi turned around to one of his aides and whispered in her ear, "Is that so?"

In a very quiet voice, she said, "Yes, sir, starting in 1985."

"It appears that we created something that we hoped would be a benefit, and now it comes back to haunt us. Ladies and gentlemen, we have spent hours here already. Thank you all." With that said, Senator Ngoi closed the meeting and stood up, followed by other committee members and exited the room. The journalists, as usual, busily texted their reports to their home offices.

Testimonies from various expert witnesses had not yielded any more information other than what had been said. Nevertheless, the Senate had shown its concern. And they had wasted many hours, half of it on their own verbosity.

Not all was lost in the day's testimonies in the Senate. As the media filed out of the room, aides for each Senator started to initiate contact with their counterparts on the UN-led committee to ask for updates on their findings.

Depending on the findings of the UN-led, super-science committee, the US Senate might hold another hearing. The House of Representatives would also investigate.

COLLECTING DNA

Three years earlier, when the Global Foundation decided to pursue the "die in good health" approach to end the wars in favor of peace, John and Dr. Roger, two of the core trustees, started to collect DNA from possible candidates for their future effort.

Collecting DNA from animals was easy; from people was a different story, difficult but not impossible.

Collecting DNA from the villagers deep in the Amazon rain forest depended on the poachers. Without the knowledge of the Brazilian government, one of the Global Foundation board members, Prof. Alvarado, hired poachers and gave them GPSs. The poachers, being poachers, simply applied their knowledge of animals to humans. When the poachers discovered some isolated populations untouched by the outside world, they were told not to make contact with the people. They were to collect materials around the village that may have been touched by the people living there. The DNA was isolated and analyzed from the surrounding plants or fecal materials. Human DNA was easily distinguished from other living materials, plants, insects and birds. The DNA from the Amazon villagers was sequenced, and the sequences were stored in computers, just as the US government had done for many citizens and government workers.

The DNA of a small number of soldiers in troublesome countries that had been in constant conflict for centuries—including Israel, Palestine, Syria, Saudi Arabia, Iran, Iraq, and Egypt—was also collected. The Global Foundation, with its vast resources, was able to insert service personnel into military camps. They were told to collect food utensils used by officers. DNA was extracted from the utensils, sequenced, and the data stored in a computer along with potential other usable DNA collected. Wet samples, i.e. the real DNA, were also stored in dry form. DNA was stable in this condition. Even some proteins could survive thousands of years. In

2015, several American scientists in California were able to isolate a protein sheet from a fossil snail thousands of years old.

In the underground laboratory in Siberia, associates of the seven Vols began to synthesize the nucleotides that suppressed the activities of genes involved in the Krebs cycle. When the computer simulation experiments were done, the scientists then sought validation with the wet samples.

After approximately one year, the simulations were accomplished. Confirmation with wet samples was accomplished in the second year.

Concomitant with the DNA research was research on the production of nanobots, with specific anti-pheromones attractants, to selected targets including the Amazon villagers, the soldiers and civilians of interest. Nanobots were synthesized with guidance systems to specific targets, and computer simulation confirmed the effectiveness.

After two years, protected from the spying eyes of satellites and the faithful associates of the seven Vols, the underground work of making nanobots with specific nucleotides and anti-pheromones could be done within two weeks. Therefore there was a two-week lead time for targeting a particular population or individuals, such as the commandos in the Israel and the Palestine arm forces. With John and Dr. Roger's input and advice, Harrison, the computer geek of the Global Foundation, was able to write programs for production using 3D-computers. Final products could be made in days. The lead time to target was shortened considerably, days instead of weeks!

Starting at the end of the twentieth century, several government agencies, including Homeland Security and the Department of Justice, had collected numerous DNA samples from individuals suspected of potential terrorism, drug trafficking and criminal activity. The DNA of well-known politicians, Senators, House members, heads of agencies, scientists, professors and industrialists were also stored somewhere. After the sequencing, their double helix sequences were kept in computers in a number of government facilities.

Retrieving DNA from the government facilities was an easy task for Harrison and his friend. They had no trouble hacking into the computers and storing the sequences; it was child's play for these two genius computer geeks.

After the death of the Israel and the Palestine commandos, the world began to take the warning statements of the Global Foundation seriously. And yet there were countries still convinced "not me or us."

China and India complied, and ceased fighting and laid off armory workers.

Russia withdrew its troops from the Ukraine border following the retreat of American ground forces. They had yet to close their armament factories.

In America, the National Rifle Association had much influence over weapons manufacturers, including builders of tanks and fighter planes. Politics in America was largely controlled by industry and business sectors. Since Israel received the most foreign aid and England was still dependent on the diplomacy of "our cousin," they pretty much followed in Uncle Sam's footsteps. Therefore, no armament factories were closed in these countries.

THE FINAL WARNING

The fourth and final warning appeared on TV stations worldwide.

"One more week's failure to close all WMD and armament factories will result in the deaths of high officials."

The USA, UK, and Israel ignored this message.

Exactly eight days from the day of the warning, five low-level deputy directors in the US government, and five CEOs of armament factories did not wake up for breakfast. In the UK, the same number of similar rank did not get up for breakfast either. Two deputy directors of Mossad also failed to wake up. All these victims died peacefully, without any symptoms, just like those in the Amazon village. Some died with smiles on their faces like they were having a good dream.

The same morning, a panel truck backed up to the apartment in New York City where Harrison and his buddy lived. Two burly guys wearing uniforms with a red *Trucking with Care* insignia on the pocket unlocked the rear doors and dropped the ramp.

Out came two boxes, a refrigerator and a dishwasher. As with a usual delivery routine, they put these appliances on the sidewalk and removed their cardboard boxes. When that was done, they went upstairs to fetch the old refrigerator and the old dishwasher. They put them in the truck. The new refrigerator and dishwasher were then carried to the apartment. All these activities were daily routines in a big city. No one paid any attention.

The truck was driven to a location with a sign that said *Reclamation Landfill, Solid Materials Only* on the East River Island. There was only one attendant there. The truck backed up to a ramp which slanted down some twenty feet into the river. There were many appliances already piled up at the end of the ramp. The two *Trucking with Care* muscles added the old refrigerator and dishwasher to others. The sole attendant then drove a tractor to the ramp after the truck had deposited the items. He then picked up piles of appliances and other rusty machines and dumped them into the murky water of the East River. Two hours later, more trucks came and the attendant again performed the same task.

No questions were asked. No forms filled out. No one paid any attention.

Inside the old refrigerator and the dishwasher removed from Harrison and his buddy's apartment were the four super-computers they had used to send out all four messages.

The best tracing programs at the top national security agencies—China's Liberation Army, the United States' CIA, Israel's Mossad, Russia's KGB and the UK's MI5—all hit a dead end; there was no data!

FINGER OFF THE TRIGGER

Since the death of American, British, and Israel officials, there had been no fighting for several months. No innocent people had been killed.

But the world leaders and the United Nations were uneasy. They were busy looking for the culprits, or bioterrorists, or peacemakers—whichever and however one wanted to categorize the events of the past several months.

Lobbyists for armament factories were also very busy. They employed a two pronged approach to keep their industries prosperous. When their government ceased to order weapons, they had to cut workers. No productions meant no sales which meant no profit. On the one hand, the lobbyists for gun manufacturers started to lobby Congress not to take the warnings seriously. They insisted that these were bioterrorists who would later demand money from Uncle Sam, essentially blackmail. They began to hire cyber-experts to trace the source or sources of the warnings. They also hired mercenaries to stand by to annihilate these bioterrorists if necessary—there were things that private citizens could do while the government was restricted by the current legal system in the United States.

When the Israeli commanders were sacrificed, Mossad began to cooperate with Arab leaders to find out how they were killed and with what. Israel had the best anti-bioterrorist capability partly due to their scientists, including a couple of Nobel Laureates at the Weisman Institute of Science. Although scientists at the Weisman Institute were not spooks, they could analyze the cells and tissues of the victims to see if there were unusual materials in or on the victim's body. In addition, they were interested in how this "poison" was applied to the victims.

The Israeli military was the most tightly organized army in the world. The number of troops was small compared to the number of Russian army troops, or the Liberation Army of China. The Israeli strength, with the superior weapons, could easily take on all the armed forces of the Middle East countries together.

The Head of Mossad, Mr. Lieberman, conferred with his deputy director. "Neither the US CDC nor the Beijing bio-warfare unit have found any traces of foreign materials in the samples from the Amazon, the fairly high-ranking deputy directors, our commandos' bodies or our colleagues; they were also unsuccessful in finding unusual materials in the bodies of the hyenas and jackals. We should look elsewhere for anomalies. We should give some samples to our scientists at the Weisman Institute. In the meantime, let us reexamine our civilian hires in recent weeks. Production of the 'poison' is one thing, delivering it is just as important."

"I have all the folders on civilian service personnel here and the units to which the victims belonged," replied the deputy director. "Last month—that would be in the right time frame—we had two service personnel, one man and one woman, who retired after fifteen years of service. The man left the country a week after retirement. His travel documents indicated he flew to Swaziland. I checked with immigration there to see if we could locate his whereabouts. Nothing. We are still on it. The woman went back to Tel Aviv to her family where she is now. I have assigned two agents to observe her daily activities."

"That is a good start," said Mr. Lieberman. "As soon as you get some results, let me know. I will be travelling to the United States, then China, to get more details in addition to what we have from the UN Security Council. You know how to reach me."

BODY ODORS AND PHEROMONES

Dr. Young and his associates from the CDC arranged a meeting with security personnel and counter-terrorist units, a rare occasion. What brought them together was not the chemistry, or search for the "poison." They wanted to find out how it was delivered to those deputy directors who lived in their homes so far away from each other. One of them had died in a hotel room in San Francisco. He was discovered when the bell boy delivered breakfast to his room. He did not answer the door, and after five minutes the bell boy called the security desk. The hotel detective used a master key to walk in. This deputy director was in bed with a smile on his face. But he could not be awakened. The 911 rescue unit rushed him to the General Hospital where he was declared dead from natural causes. That meant they did not know why and how he perished.

The body was shipped to the CDC in Atlanta. Other bodies were also shipped to Atlanta as soon as the deaths were discovered. Two of the deputy directors had been in bed with their wives—one could imagine the sudden shock of finding their husbands unresponsive to their touches.

Executives and mid-level officials in the UK and Israel died in the same manner.

After a round of shaking hands and introducing each other, Dr. Young began the discussions: "Mr. Lieberman, thank you for coming. I hope, putting together with all information from the intelligence communities, to come up with some solution. At least we can formulate a plan to find out who the perpetrators are and how the poison was delivered."

"Thank you, Dr. Young. Gentlemen, I will summarize the findings made by our security agency and scientists at the Weisman Institute. I will then report to you what we are doing."

Mr. Lieberman continued, "As you may guess, the Weisman Institute had the same results as yours—that is, they came up empty handed. There are no clues as to why these officials and commandos were unable to wake up. Some of them died with a smile on their faces as if they were dreaming, which is sad. Now allow me to tell you another approach. We are now concentrating our efforts on discovering how the murderous agents were delivered. In our barracks, we hire civilians for general services such as cooks and kitchen help. During the timeframe when these soldiers were killed, two kitchen helps, one male and one female, retired. We replaced them with two new hires. The male retiree left for Swaziland one week after the death of the soldiers. The woman went back to her family in Tel Aviv. Two agents are watching her activities. So far, we have not found the man. Our agents are searching, so are Swaziland's agents.

"It appears that all the victims, including those in the Amazon, died within hours of receiving the infectious agent or agents. We believe if we find out how the "poison" was delivered and administered, that would be the first step to find the perpetrators. We have studied reports of every kind. Does that sound like a reasonable plan?"

"In view of the lack of biological data, it is certainly a logical next step," said the representative from the CIA.

"Mr. Lieberman," asked the representative from the US Homeland Security, "you said the retirees were kitchen helps. Did you check the utensils used the night before the soldier died? Also what were your soldiers doing the evening before their death?"

"Yes, we did. There was nothing unusual. The kitchen help and service personnel performed their usual duties of serving and cleaning, and then left."

"Were they searched when they came into the compound?" asked the FBI agent.

"Yes, for weapons, just like we do in our airports—there was nothing out of the ordinary except—."

Everyone perked up their ears.

"Except—the man came to the camp wearing a scarf. The guards noticed nothing unusual about the woman. We have monitors at the gate. We kept the tapes for one week, not twenty-four hours. That was the only time this male help wore a scarf to work. We are looking for that scarf and the man. When we find this man in Swaziland, or elsewhere, we certainly will ask him about the scarf."

"Do you think the scarf may have been a vehicle for the agent that killed the soldiers?" asked Dr. Young.

"It is possible."

"How about on the Palestine side?" asked the FBI agent.

"They don't have service personnel," replied Mr. Lieberman. "They themselves do the chores. They do have local kids doing errands. Anyone could have hired one of these urchins to carry things into the barracks."

"How about the other people who died?" asked the FBI agent.

"We checked. Nothing unusual, including the mail delivery—nothing."

Dr. Young spoke up. "There is a uniqueness about this 'poison.' It appears to be person-specific. It did not affect the wives sleeping next to their husbands. It did not affect other soldiers in the same barracks. It targeted only ten commanders out of several hundred. And you all know about the hyenas and the jackals. No other animals were affected."

The man from the CIA frowned. "Dr. Young, I understand the species of animals. Hyenas are not jackals. But humans are different."

"Yes," nodded Dr. Young. "Humans belong to one species, *Homo sapiens*. However, there are sub-species and races, such as Caucasian and Negroid. We in this room have our own set of genes, although we all carry human genes. These genes are common to all—genes for pigment, for example, differ from individual to individual. All of us here have different pigments."

Mr. Lieberman looked excited. "Dr. Young, are you thinking what I am thinking? That is, the perpetrator(s) knew about the DNA of all the victims and collected them?"

"I can answer that," interjected Kirby, assistant to Dr. Young. "Male and female hormones are different. All of us have different pheromones, like all of us have different body odors. The perpetrator must have known our DNA which is the code for everything in our body, including body odors."

"So the perpetrator makes an agent targeting a particular individual, like some cancer drugs targeting particular cancer cells?" asked the FBI Special Agent.

"How did they know about their DNA?" asked the CIA agent.

The Director of Homeland Security explained: "There is a large repertoire of DNA for all government workers above Grade 12. That would correspond to manager or above. A thirteen-year-old hacked into the repertoire once. He got caught because he was bragging about it to his classmates. His teacher reported it to us. If he did it, so can other cyber-geniuses. I suspect that was how these perpetrators got the DNA sequences of the now-dead officials, and worked from there, probably including your soldiers, Mr. Lieberman."

"And the others?" Mr. Lieberman asked. "Assuming the perpetrators can do all this, there is still a problem in making the 'poison' specific to one individual. Another problem is the carrier system." He paused and continued. "Pheromone or body odor specific?"

"My God!" exclaimed Dr. Young's assistant, Kirby. "We have done this for insects in the sixties here in California. A company in California synthesized a pheromone-like substance to attract fruit flies so they would not go to the orchards. Instead, they went to the trap. That saved the California orchard farmers millions of dollars!"

PEACE AT HAND?

On a sunny late autumn day, some of the leaves in Central Park started to lose their green pigment. It was a signal to New Yorkers to drive up to the New England states to see the fall colors. On that particular day, Mr. Erikson stood at the front door of the Global Foundation to greet the board members, only the core members. They held the meeting in the Faraday cage in the basement of the building, since this room was soundproof and protected from electromagnetic fields.

Once all core board members had settled, Mr. Erikson said: "We have much to discuss. As you know, our task has been successful, so far. There has been no war in the past several months. Can that go on? Is peace at hand?"

John, the scientist from the big AZ pharma, was first to give an update. "We cannot be optimistic at this time—it is still early. From all my contacts in DC, every national security agency and the CDC, the NIH, as well as the Walter Reed General Hospital has appointed Special Forces to deal with the situation. The UN Security Council has set aside a weekly meeting to collate information from all the agencies concerned. Our Senate also has a special committee looking into the matter and is asking for findings from the UN committee. Mr. Lieberman of the Israeli Mossad was in Atlanta with the special task force appointed by the White House, and representatives of appropriate department heads of the CIA, FBI, NSA, and Homeland Security. Oh, yes, the National Rifle Association is involved too."

Mr. Erikson added, "For the first time, friends and foes are not only talking to each other but also exchanging information—such as the Israelis and their neighbors in the Middle East. I don't think their unusual cooperation is aiming for peace. I think they are all trying to solve the problem, i.e. to find us."

"That is true," agreed Mr. Shum. "Their approach and their working hypothesis may be on track. I have put listening devices in the rooms where some of them stay, although the information may be sketchy—not much and not useful."

"They all stayed at your hotels? How did you manage that?" asked Ms. Layug.

"It's not hard; all the hotels participate in a government discount program. I do better, I upgrade with the same government discount as others. There are no written documents, just word of mouth. A suite is easier to bug and it's good for my business too," said Mr. Shum without much expression, as usual.

"I assume you have recorded some conversations," said Mr. Kennedy.

"Yes. I think we can construct a fairly clear picture from the partial and casual conversations. There is nothing of value from Mr. Lieberman—he just asked room service for kosher meals."

Mr. Shum inserted the disc into a disc player and pushed the play button. They all leant forward to listen to the bugged conversations.

—This Lieberman from Israel is smart—has to be, he is the head honcho of Mossad—I think the woman from CDC is smart too—She narrowed it down to pheromones like body odors, what a comparison—Right. So, Joe, want to go down for a drink before bed?—

"That was in the suite occupied by two CIA agents," said Mr. Shum. "They had a separate suite. Obviously they talked a little before they had a drink."

—I told our director about not storing DNA sequences in a computer. Just keep that damn DNA in vials. They are harder to steal—A thirteen-year-old kid hacked into the computers, got caught—a big mouth he was—we would not know if he didn't—gene jockeys, that's what they are called, they can pull genes out or something like that---pheromone genes too?—

"That was from the two FBI agents," said Mr. Shum.

—Soldiers in Israel and Palestine, hired help can be bought—easy—Lieberman is looking for a guy with a scarf—he will find him. Mossad has more tentacles than an octopus—right—got some drink here—no, let's go to the bar—

"This was from Homeland Security guys," said Mr. Shum.

"Mr. Shum, you are a good spook," smiled Ms. Layug.

"No, Ms. Layug. I just have contacts and the means."

"Anything on Harrison's computers?" asked Mr. Erikson.

"No. What you heard is all I have recorded."

Mr. Kennedy nodded and added, "Like the UN Security Council, they all have 'no data.' We dumped Harrison's gears into the East River afterward. So far, we are safe on this."

"But they are on the right track of DNA and pheromones," said John.

"John, are all your scientist colleagues and their associates back to their jobs?" asked Mr. Erikson.

"Yes. And Ms. Jankovic and Mr. Sonnovovitch have sanitized the lab in Siberia. It is back to the original condition. Mr. Chuen Lo did a great job."

"By the way, DJ too," added Mr. Kennedy. "DJ, where did the construction and maintenance workers go?"

"Well, I bought them off, sort of," DJ replied. "They and their families have been relocated. Some went back to their villages with a lot of money. Two went to America; their children are in college there. Two went to New Zealand. I have complete trust in them. They worked for me for more than twenty years. They don't know exactly where they were, just some idea. Ms. Jankovic did a great job making sure they did not see the surroundings while they were on vacation during the two and half years. That also applied to John's scientist associates."

Ms. Jankovic added, "My relatives and their wives have gone back to Serbia. I also gave them enough money to open stores and the like. We in Serbia treasure our relatives. No problem there."

John continued, "We have developed the procedures. It is now a routine. Any one of my Tennessee friends can produce them within a couple of weeks in their labs if needed. Of course, we can do that in days here with the 3-D printers. They will not involve their associates. During the work in Shelter 113, complete protocols were not written down. What we did was give each associate a particular task. My associates assembled them into nanobots. We did consider using micro-drones as a delivery system but we cannot make drones without some metals, so that was out. In five years, we may be able to make micro-drones with silicon or even digestible proteins, but we cannot wait that long."

"Did they all go back to their labs, John?" asked Ms. Layug.

"Five retired, took early retirement. They are in their mid-forties. The other four took an extended leave of absence. We paid them well enough to be comfortable for the rest of their lives. Two went to South America and opened tourist hotels. I don't think they will talk. It would be extremely difficult for the authorities to tie them to our project. Many thanks to you, Ms. Layug and Harrison, for being able to able to 'delete' certain people from the list of 'possible people of interest' in the computers of both the CIA and FBI. Also, you and your psychologists did a great job vetting them."

"One came to my lab," said Dr. Roger.

"We have so far accomplished our goals but it is not over yet," cautioned Mr. Kennedy. "We still have to be careful. Carry on our routines. By the way, Harrison and his friend have moved. They are now regular staff. They are over-qualified but we buy whatever toys they want for their hobbies."

"They are good kids," said Ms. Layug.

"Mr. Sonnovovitch, is there any talk in Moscow?" asked Mr. Erikson.

Mr. Sonnovovitch consulted his notes before replying. "Our new KGB is working with the Arabs and Iranians, and the Chinese too. So far they have no leads—it's a dead end at the computers. We are better at cyber-espionage than the Americans but not the Chinese. The Chinese have traced Harrison to the state of New York, but not New York City. I don't think they will dredge the East River."

He continued, "On the biological side, no one has yet mentioned pheromone or nanobot. The Russians obtained that from the Atlanta meetings."

"For once, the UN is leading the investigation. I don't know if it is good or bad for us," said Dr. Roger, looking worried.

"We shall wait and see how long they can keep their hands off their guns. At least we have saved many lives in the past several months. Let's hope we can save more and more," said Ms. Layug.

"Maybe we can make this an annual event, i.e. get rid of a couple corrupt officials as warnings. Terrorize them once in a while, make them keep their fingers off the triggers," suggested Mr. Erikson.

"We have to be vigilant," warned John. "We need to use all our contacts for feedback in the event we need to deal with them. Remember one of my graduate school buddies, Jack the US Marine? He is keeping his eyes and ears open at the Pentagon. For now, the armed forces are not involved. In time they will be—and they have very good scientists, like Jerry. Remember him? He is in the army."

"John, I am very impressed with your graduate school friends," said Dr. Roger. "Maybe we should recruit more like them. Harvard should have a football team like the Volunteers. With all the years I have been in Cambridge, I have not encountered those like your Vols, John." Dr. Rogers.

"Thank you, Dr. Rogers."

"We have a number of staff who will retire soon. Mr. Kennedy, make sure they receive good pensions," said Mr. Erikson.

Mr. Shum chimed in with a generous offer. "All of them and their families can stay free, for one week, at one of my resort hotels anywhere. Ms. Layug, would you help me with that? Here are the names of several of my trusted associates at various locations in the world. I have told them you will contact them for the retiring staff and their families."

Mr. Shum handed Ms. Layug a piece of paper with names on it.

"I will take care of their transportation," said Ms. Jankovic.

She continued, "They can travel on the Trans-Siberian passenger train. If you have not done so, you all should do it if you have time. We have just upgraded the equipment too."

"That is very generous of you, Ms. Jankovic," said DJ of Beijing.

"Isn't this what Americans call a fringe benefit?" said Ms. Jankovic, jokingly.

"Ladies and gentlemen, just one more piece of business," John continued. "Remember Jack and Jerry who are practical and have military backgrounds? Some time ago they asked us what if someone, anyone, including us here, decided to drop out of the program, and carelessly revealed our secret. How would we ensure that would not happen? If it did happen, how would we deal with it? It is a pessimistic thought but it could happen. We all hope it won't."

"Yes. We must not forget that," said Mr. Erikson.

Ms. Layug addressed John with a question: "John, can your friends come up with some physical or biological means to ensure no leak? Then we can assess the possibilities in the personal angle for the possibility."

"Let us think this through and discuss via email," concluded Mr. Erikson. "We have been friends and colleagues with the same conviction. Now is the time we actually need to be frank and open-minded."

There was no disagreement.

The board adjourned, but not without a cautious mode of mind.

The Global Foundation continued its routine rescue missions.

SECOND WHITE HOUSE MEETING

In the Oval Office, the President picked up a phone, pushed a key, and said, "I want a meeting, tomorrow if the schedule allows, one hour max, for the following people: The Joint Chief of Staff, the Director of our National Science Foundation, the Director of the National Institute of Health and Human Services, the Chief of staff at Walter Reed, my science adviser, the Director of CDC in Atlanta, Dr. Young, the VPs of R&D of the two largest pharmaceutical firms, division chief of bioterrorism of Homeland Security, and the Secretaries of State and Defense."

At 6 A.M. EST the following morning, the President walked into the meeting room. "Good morning everyone," he said.

"Good morning, Mr. President," they echoed in unison.

The President wasted no time starting the meeting. "Please be seated. Thank you for coming. Before I meet with of the leaders of China, Russia, UK, France, Germany, Japan, Africa Union, at the UN day after tomorrow, I want your briefings, recent progress, and assessment of our 'killings' here and abroad. Dr. Young, would you summarize your meetings in Atlanta?"

"Yes, Mr. President. I shall be brief. We still have no evidence or data as to what this 'poison' is. We did however narrow down the methodology. The perpetrators based it on the production on DNA. They obtained DNA from the Amazon villagers. They must have hacked into our DNA repertoire to gain access to the DNA sequence of our officials. This agent or agents were encapsulated, most likely, in nanobots or drones. That is about all."

"Dr. Kaighn, are there studies relative to this sort of research at the NIH?"

Dr. Kaighn, director of the NIH, was a lanky gentleman of sixty. He was a musician before he was a scientist. He was probably the most persevering scientist in the field of cell culture. He developed many culture systems for basic as well as applied biology, such as making artificial skin for grafts.

"Yes, Mr. President. Dr. Ting and his associates have been working on putting specific cancer drugs into nanobots which have a targeting macromolecule in certain cancer cells. But it will be at least another year before we have clinical trials."

"Dr. Ebert, are there grant proposals in recent months or years relative to this?"

"Yes, Mr. President. Related to NIH studies, there are three proposals to coat nanobots with pheromones from fruit flies, locust and corn bores. The purposes are to encapsulate insecticides into the nanobots coated with species-specific pheromones to target these organisms without affecting other beneficial insects in the same environment."

"Any positive result?"

"No, sir, we just granted their proposals at the last grant review two months ago."

"General Carl, I recall that there was a similar study or more appropriately, similar approach in the germ warfare division, some years back when I was at Yale. Is that correct?"

"Yes, Mr. President. We are trying to identify a set of genes that can slow down metabolism. The goal is to make soldiers lazy on the front line—not our soldiers of course. We then will have the advantage in combat."

"General, that is ingenious. Please keep me informed on it every three months."

"Dr. Smith of Star Pharm and Dr. Jones, you two are in the private sector. When you leave, please keep all we discuss to yourselves. I trust your discretion."

"Of course, Mr. President," answered Dr. Smith and Dr. Jones in unison.

Dr. Jones was John, one of the Vols. He was VP of R&D of AZ Pharma.

"Please tell us the latest dealing with drug delivery system and treatment at the DNA level—Dr. Smith first."

Dr. Smith cleared his throat. "Yes, Mr. President. At our firm, we use the latest technique called CRISPR-Cas 9 methodology to break up DNA. Then we look for sequences that may be related to diabetes, prostate cancer and heart diseases. Interestingly, we found a stretch that control respiration, precisely, rate of respiration. That was unexpected. Now we put this finding along with other studies and ask, 'Why do we need to sleep?'"

"Dr. Jones?"

"Yes, Mr. President. We are researching the means to deliver specific drugs to specific cells. Instead of nanobots, we are researching the use of drones, microdrones."

"Dr. Jones, Dr. Smith, and General Carl, your studies appear to me to be in the same ball park. Is that so?"

The President paused for a second, allowing General Carl, Dr. Jones and Dr. Smith to gather their thoughts. He was not a scientist; however, he was able to distill many facts into a salient whole. And that was a presidential quality.

After a lapse of a minute or so, all three gentlemen did agree with the President.

"Dr. Jones, on drones or microdrones, what kind of materials are being tested if you are at that stage of research?" asked the President.

"We are now using silicon, molecular silicon, micro latex and proteins."

"Which material, among these three, is digestible with natural occurring enzymes in our cells?" asked the President.

"Only protein, Mr. President."

"How far along are you at this moment?"

"We estimate a year for silicon and latex; for protein, two to three," replied Dr. Jones.

The President looked worried. "In critical times and for critical issues, government and private sectors must come together to solve the problems. I believe we are now facing it. Dr. Smith and Dr. Jones, would you talk to your respective CEOs about sharing data or having discussions with us? I don't really know how scientists work. I don't want to use my executive power yet. But I think it will be good for all. I really don't want this to fall into the wrong hands. Dr. Carlson, what do you make out of this weird death without symptoms?"

"Mr. President, I am sorry that this is the first time for us too. We have had no patients with similar deaths at Walter Reed. I have also checked with Boston General, San Francisco General and MD Anderson in Texas—none."

"If these weird deaths occur again, and if we can catch it in time, would you be able to, hypothetically, diagnose and treat the 'disease'?"

"Sir, I cannot make any statement, hypothetically or theoretically." Dr. Carlson was very practical.

The President rubbed his left temple, obviously collecting this thoughts. "Gentlemen, let me try to draw a picture. Please fill in the blanks. From the discussions with the UN Security Council, the meeting in Atlanta and this morning, it seems that the perpetrator or perpetrators have successfully developed a method or 'poison' targeting a particular sequence in our DNA. They were able to deliver this 'poison'—perhaps bioweapon is a better description—to target a person or persons in a crowd. And this bioweapon is undetectable with known technology. Gentlemen, frankly, I am scared. And yet, I am glad we are travelling on the same road. We, with international effort, need to cooperate and pool our data and brain juice. And remember, our Senate is deeply involved too. That is good."

There were affirmative nods all around.

"General Carl, would you head up a consortium, a scientific consortium with our top scientists in academia, as well as the private sector to study this bioweapon and develop a possible counter-measure. And each will appoint one or two members in an advisory role. And, by the way, I want all members and associates to be native-born Americans, and to have no intimate contact or interaction with any foreign concerns. And I want to emphasize, we have to protect the scientists and their families from undue harm." The President looked at General Carl.

"Yes, Mr. President. It is my honor."

The outcome of this meeting was clear in that the President was able to grasp the gist of the event and determine how to go forward to resolve the problem at hand. His approach for a solution was not political—a first in American politics.

UNITED NATIONS GENERAL ASSEMBLY

The world had been without bullets flying through the air for more than six months now. Tanks were not rumbling on the ground, and the air was devoid of fighter planes, bombers and missiles. There had been no killings of innocent men, women, and children by bombing the so-called ISIS strongholds which at the moment were inactive. The only waves being made were by fishing boats and cruise ships, not war ships, on the ocean. There were no refugees fleeing from their war-torn homes because there were no wars. On average there were zero civilians killed, compared with two to three hundred thousand during the same periods in previous years. Isolated instances of violence did happen here and there.

The Global Foundation had accomplished its goal, and the world was at peace.

So it seemed…

There was an undercurrent of turmoil in the economic sector of all the industrial nations in the northern hemisphere. When the arms factories were closed and the workers laid off, many corollary businesses took a dive too. Steel mills laid off workers. Overstocked copper mines closed, driving the price of metal lower than ever. Chemical companies that made cordite also followed the downhill trend. Petroleum industries, both crude and refineries, had to furlough many. Governments had to deal with the problem of unemployment and associated social unhealthiness related to unemployment.

Was this peace or an illusion of peace?

Or a price paid for the sake of peace?

Did the Trustees of the Global Foundation and the Vols now face the dilemma of creating bad by doing good?

In the meantime, the United Nations was leading a drive to uncover how the chosen victims were killed and by whom.

For the first time since its inception in San Francisco in 1945, the annual UN General Assembly was attended by all the world leaders with their science advisors. Manhattan was congested with limousines and security personnel, both local permanent and temporary visitors.

The day before the UN annual meeting, the President of the United States picked up the phone, pushed a button and said "I want to include Dr. Young of the CDC to attend the UN General Assembly in Manhattan the day after tomorrow."

"Yes, sir," came the answer on the other end of the phone.

The weather in New York City on the day of the assembly matched the mood of the heads of states and their diplomats—gloomy!

Instead of the usually diplomatic cheerfulness, even if only on the surface, this time the mood was somber because of the inability to find a single thread of evidence by all the elite institutions throughout the world as to what had caused the sacrificial deaths.

When all the protocols were over, hands shaken, shoulders patted, leaders of the world took their seats with their aids sitting behind them.

The Secretary of the UN, Mr. Tonga of Uganda, stood up, smiled pleasantly, and gave his welcome speech. "Welcome to you all. As you know, we are in a very unusual situation at this moment. About six months ago, a large population of hyenas and jackals were singled out to be killed in Africa. A couple of weeks later, a hundred or so villagers in the Amazon rain forest, then soldiers in the Middle East, officials in the US, the UK and Israel, died in the similar manner as the animals—with no obvious symptoms. They died in good health?! Then came the warnings, the origin of which none of us have been able to trace, let alone the perpetrators. We have complied with the warnings. We stopped the battles and borderline conflicts. It has been good in that there have been no civilian casualties of wars because there have been no wars. The goal of this United Nations established after World War II, in October 1945, was to prevent future conflicts. As we know, we have not done so although we have done many good deeds: With the work of UNESCO and the World Health Organization we have raised the standard of living for many, and educated numerous populations who otherwise would not have the chance.

"Although there has been no major war like World War II, minor conflicts only ceased six months ago. That was not because of us so we cannot take the credit. Some unknown organization, or organizations, have employed tactics of terrorism to "blackmail" countries at war—I am not sure if it is the right or wrong terminology. Innocent people and harmless animals were sacrificed to send us the message. Whether it is right or wrong, each of us may see it from a different angle or view it through a different filter. Nevertheless, the underlying fact presents a danger. The perpetrators' technology of creating such a deadly agent—I assume there is a physical agent—is beyond our current knowledge. The delivery system has also escaped us. We also have not been able to find from whom and where those messages came.

"The underlying danger, and I must emphasize this, is what if this highly sophisticated bioweapon gets into the wrong hands? What if their targets are those of us sitting here? Their messages and their actions have demonstrated that they are indeed capable in targeting us.

"Could it be the right way to prevent conflicts, the original goal of the United Nations? We must find out who they are. We know the why.

"We are not at peace. We live under the illusion of peace. Our economies have declined and it has led to the beginning of a new societal ill-being because of mass unemployment. I do not perceive this as peace or peaceful.

"We, all of us in this room, should and will cooperate to find a solution, a scientific solution to search and find these perpetrators, obviously a group of very talented scientists. I will emphasize again, we will not permit this technology to fall into the wrong hands.

"If I may, I shall end with a quote from Dr. Henry Kissinger, but with a different punctuation mark, 'Peace is at hand?'

"Since 1945, US President Roosevelt conceived this very organization of the United Nations, the United States of America has been the most generous host for us in many ways. Please welcome the President of the United States of America." With that said, Secretary General Tonga ended his welcoming remarks.

As usual, there was polite applause. But the somber mood of all in the auditorium could be felt by even the most amateurish person in geopolitics.

The President of United States stood about six feet tall, with broad shoulders and of medium build. Although there were no obvious discernable wrinkles on his face, he walked up to the podium with a heavy heart and the weight of the world on his shoulders. The UN General Assembly was usually just pleasant, political speech from world leaders.

Not today.

The President of United States carried a thin blue folder with the emblem of the United States of America on the front. He put it on the podium but did not open it.

"Mr. Tonga, fellow leaders of nations, ladies and gentlemen, the current event has resulted in the absence of bullets flying overhead. Many lives are still with us. However, with this obvious change in the world, there is an underlying future that may not be optimistic. I fully agree with Mr. Tonga that there is danger lurking in the future. I further agree with Mr. Tonga that this moment with no wars may be just an illusion of peace. Not real peace—just a temporary peacefulness on the surface.

"The governing of nations changes with time. Concomitant with these changes are living standards. Since the end of World War II, the Korean and Vietnam conflicts, the Russia-Ukraine conflict, and religious wars in the Middle East, there have been no wars near the scale of those mentioned above. Most of us have lived without fear of a World War III. Global realpolitik has changed—there has been a change in world order, a change for the better. Territorial expansion as the means to pursue national security has diminished compared with, for example, Japan in the twentieth century and Russia in the seventeenth century. The reunification of East Germany and West Germany was the nucleus of prosperity in Europe. The unification of North and South Korea has stabilized the Pacific Rim with the balance of power. There is now a new world order of peace, still with a question mark, however.

"We all agree nuclear power has been better used to generate energy rather than generate the mass death of humanity. Other than a small number of nations lacking nuclear weapons, we all possess them but have not and will not use them. This nuclear capability epitomizes the balance of power.

"A balance of power in the long run will give us peace. The use of raw, superior power, both economic and military, will not.

"Our advance in computer technology and biotechnology has given us physical health of a level unimaginable fifty years ago. We can now cure some diseases that we were not able to cure fifty years ago. Fifty years ago, we could treat the symptoms of diabetes. Now, we can cure it at the DNA level—no more daily injection of insulin. We can correct the genes for hemoglobin abnormality such as sickle-cell anemia, thalassemia, and other genetic diseases, such as Tay-Sachs disease. Yes, cancer remains our biggest challenge. But we are not far from winning the war on cancer, at least some of it, and many other deadly diseases. Soon we will be able to target cancer cells without affecting normal cells nearby, with the use of robots, precisely, nano-robotic technology to deliver specific drugs.

"Robots and nanotechnology can benefit humankind. Unfortunately, they can also harm us. For example, the definition of defense or offense weapons depends on which direction the barrels of guns are pointing.

"With a heavy heart, nevertheless, I must praise those scientists, and whoever is behind their achievement in developing such advanced methodology as the euthanasia of animal and fellow human beings without a trace of distress.

"I concur completely with Mr. Tonga in that this technology could become weapon of mass destruction. All of us realize the chance of such possibility. Therefore, we have pooled our resources to try to trace the origin. We have no answer at this moment. But that does not mean we will not find one soon.

"I admit that the United States of America has the largest arms production and best innovation in weaponry in the world. Because of this, our economy is also suffering more than any other nation. The people of the United States of America will gladly sacrifice some comfort and luxury living for the good of the world. Any economist will tell us that it is not just the arms; there are many other businesses, industries and labor forces affected. Globalization has been in full throttle since the year 2000. The effect on one country will affect others on earth, some more seriously than others.

"We have brought together the most talented scientists among us. They will have a biotechnology super summit to find a resolution. We will make sure that this advanced technology will not fall into the wrong hands. Thank you."

A standing ovation and loud applause were given to the President of the United States of America.

The President shook hands with Mr. Tonga.

At the end of a series of speeches by world leaders, Mr. Tonga shook hands with all the delegates on the stage. The delegates then walked down to the aisles and shook hands with various people in the audience.

POST UN ASSEMBLY

John, the leader of the Seven Vols and VP of R&D with a prominent pharmaceutical firm, AZ Inc. was in the audience at the UN General Assembly. While the President of United States was shaking hands, he looked around as a diplomat and politician usually did. He paused in front of John, took a second look and said, "You looked familiar. But forgive me—"

"Mr. President, I am John with—"

"Yes, I remember, you received a Medal of Freedom two years ago. Dr. Jones. Correct?"

"Yes, Mr. President, my pleasure again."

They shook hands.

"Dr. Jones," said the President said, and waved to Dr. Young. "Dr. Young, let me introduce Dr. Jones, one of the recipients of a Medal of Freedom two years ago. Do you know each other?"

"Only by reputation, Mr. President," replied John.

"Same here, Mr. President," said Dr. Young.

They shook hands.

"You are both scientists, actually molecular biologists, am I correct?"

"Yes, Mr. President." John and Dr. Young spoke almost in unison.

"I want you both to join a special committee I have appointed to deal with the problem," said the President and nodded to one of his aides. He then continued down the aisle followed by his aides, shaking hands with a presidential smile.

"Dr. Young, good to know you. We will be seeing each other soon," said John said as he looked at his watch. "I am late to meet my wife somewhere on Fifth Avenue. I promised to go shopping with her then a show. We don't come east often. That is togetherness. She never wants to go along to meetings with me. Today is different.

I am more or less on vacation, on the orders of my boss—both at home and at work."

"Dr. Jones."

"Call me John."

"And I am Donald," said Dr. Young. "We all know who our real boss is—be seeing you."

John headed out the door while Dr. Young returned to the entourage from the White House.

ORCHID GARDEN HOTEL

As soon as he entered his hotel room and took off his tie after the UN assembly meeting and shopping, John flipped his Notebook open and started to email the other Vols. The message was simple, in encrypted format.

"Friends, we need to meet again ASAP. There is a molecular/cell biology conference in Boston next week. I will be giving a lecture at MIT during that week. After that, there will be a Gordon Research Conference. Mr. Shum has a hotel in Boston. I do not recall the name at this moment. You will receive details from Harrison soon, very soon."

Because of the timing and what had happened recently, almost everyone who owned a flat screen TV was watching the UN General Assembly, which had never had such a large audience.

Until now.

The scientists from the land of Volunteers watched it too.

Each of them had a similar emotional reaction. When they received John's encrypted emails, they all knew what they would discuss in a few days' time in Boston.

Jack was to drive to Boston from D.C. Jim and others would fly in. Since they did not reside in the same city, they would arrive at Logan International Airport at different times.

The Orchid Garden Hotel had two entrances for guests, and in the back one for deliveries and employees. The front door was large and ornate with motifs of flowers, namely orchids. The rotating glass doors were fifteen feet of glass and stainless steel adorned with ten-inch door knobs. One just had to touch the door knob and the rotating door would rotate slowly allowing the guests to walk into the lobby. This architectural design was uniquely different from most designs for hotels. Limos and taxis dropped guests at the curb which was some forty feet from the main door.

The side door around the corner was another entrance, not as large but just as beautiful. The wide sidewalk curved around to the east side of the hotel. This side entrance was mainly for departing guests. Even with hundreds or more people going in and out, there was no congestion, busy but not crowded. It was not like monster hotels-casinos in Las Vegas where one had to dodge cars, guests and bellboys.

This marvelous hotel with every room facing or partially facing the Boston harbor was also designed by the architecture firm of E & E, the twin sisters. They had become Mr. Shum's friends and architects.

There were surveillance cameras at every entrance. The recordings would be stored on designated computers. If so desired, one could view all recordings as far back as one week. At times, there would be glitches, like all high-tech gadgets. These monitors were not really protected from hacking because of the lack of really confidential information. Cyber jockeys like Harrison of the Global Foundation could easily hack in and change the recorded data, if needed.

Unless there was a disturbance, large or small, at an entrance to the Orchid Garden Hotel, the security tapes were never rewound to see who came through the doors. Additionally, there were security personnel disguised as clerks in the lobby, and porters at the delivery entrance. Some of the greeters and hospitality workers in the lobbies were also on double duty as security personnel.

When the Vol friends stepped into the lobby with a ceiling some six stories high with a glass dome looking at the open sky, they were chaperoned to an elevator apart from the bank of guest elevators. It was discreetly isolated from the others behind a waterfall. They rode up to the penthouse, Mr. Shum's private residence.

John was in the penthouse of the Orchid Garden Hotel when his conspirators, the Volunteer friends, arrived. The mood and atmosphere were unlike their previous meetings. They were somber. But as usual they all were happy to see each other.

Without unnecessary introductory remarks, John said, "We know why we are gathered here again in Boston. We all heard what our President said. He and Mr. Tonga were correct. If our technology falls into the wrong hands, it certainly will be a WMD. At this time, we are the only ones who know how to put it together."

He took a sip of water and continued: "There is also a very unusual request from the President. You may remember I received a Medal of Freedom two years ago. I was in the audience at the UN recently but I did not think I would bump into the President. As he walked down the aisle, he somehow spotted me and recognized me. He introduced me to Dr. Young, a Nobel laureate, I think you know who he is. I only know Dr. Young by reputation. He was with the President's entourage. The President wanted me to serve in a special committee with Dr. Young to quote 'deal with this problem' unquote."

There was silence. The mood in the penthouse was like the atmosphere in the Amazon, ninety degrees Fahrenheit with a hundred percent humidity, no rain!

"This was not unexpected. I am sure it has been in the back of our minds since the last reunion in Manhattan," said Ruth.

"We had to weigh the benefit against the harm," said Jack. "Technically, it will be developed sooner or later. We just joined together and did it sooner. By-passing proprietary and government confidential information, we are just five years ahead."

"Jim's pheromone and Harold's DNA triple-strand approach would not have been merged if they had gone to different grad schools, or even at different times in Knoxville," said Jerry.

"That probably applied to all of us," said John.

June nodded her agreement. "Our research accomplishment would not have been at this level if it we had not kept in contact with each other. We have shared data that is not supposed to be shared. We have not done that openly of course. Little hints here and little numbers there have helped all of us. For 'this,' as our President put it, we put our heads together."

Jim added, "We had the best associates to do the work too. And the best instruments money can buy. With Harrison's help, we shortened the time from five years to two and half."

"I need some advice. How do we proceed from here?" asked John.

"John, you are in a pretty precarious position," warned Harold. "For us civilians, we just go back to our jobs and keep our mouths shut. Jack and Jerry will just follow orders."

"I know. I am sure there is a way if we put our heads together again," said John. "Let us break for lunch," he said and then pushed a button on the phone.

Fifteen minutes later, Mr. Shum's trusted manager and a waiter exited the private elevator. They pushed out two carts with food. Various drinks were in the well-stocked refrigerators in the kitchen. They put some food on the kitchen counter and left some on the carts. The manager shook hands with John.

Before the manager left, he handed John a handful of room key cards with instructions.

Lunch was fit for a king. But the seven Vols ate with heavy hearts. They were facing a dilemma, unlike the dilemma they had when they first met some three years ago to initiate this humanity project with sacrificial lambs, including human. They did not expect the world would have such strong reactions. They did not expect the UN would organize the hunt for them with the US President leading the pack.

Most unexpected was that John was invited to join the hunters' pack. John could not refuse and would be working with the best molecular biologists in the world on the hunt. This special UN-led super-science committee had almost total support from the world. The only region that did not want to participate was the Middle East. Even at this time of prosperity, religion still dominated politics there. There had not been the ideology of the separation of church and state in known history. Church and state were one and the same in the Middle East—no Westphalian concept there.

Confucius once said, "People can move mountains and redirect the flow of the mighty Yangtze, but people cannot change their innate character."

BALANCE OF POWER

After lunch the Vols relaxed a bit and talked about old times in Knoxville before they resumed the discussion. Their mood had not changed. The atmosphere in this magnificent penthouse, overlooking the Boston Harbor, was still like under the canopy in the Amazon—humid, stuffy and hot.

John was pacing around the dining room. He called the manager to bring more fresh coffee and remove the dishes and the leftover lunch. Within minutes the manager and the same waiters arrived and did their work.

John again shook hands with the manager, who said: "Dr. Jones, Mr. Shum left instructions that you can use the penthouse for as long as you need. He and his family will not need it for another two months. All the rooms are complimentary. We always keep a block of suites vacant, just in case, for special needs. Just check out as usual at the desk. Please return the key cards, they are sort of special. If there is anything you need, please just call." The manager and waiters left.

"Mr. Shum is certainly very generous," said Ruth.

"Ruth, he probably has more money than God!" said Harold.

"For your information," said John, "he has willed fifty percent of his wealth to our Foundation and the other half to his children. Mr. Kennedy estimated that the Foundation can keep on functioning for another five years in the black, even without contributions from anyone else."

"That doesn't seem real," said Jim.

"Real or not, Mr. Shum is one of a kind. He never questions what we do or how we do it. He does know why and comes to board meetings. Let's get back to work."

Looking pensive, Harold looked said, "John, I was thinking over lunch. Maybe we should just hand the techniques to UNESCO and let the United Nations give it to everyone. This idea came to me when I was looking over the cold-cut plates. They were appetizing as well as beautifully arranged, in a harmonious pattern. When we eat as few as we have, the balance and the harmony of beauty is ruined.

"Most of the countries have had nuclear weapons since the mid-1900. Back then, even poor Pakistan did. Although conditions of the surrender of Japan prohibited Japan from having nuclear weapons, but that did not apply to nuclear power plants. Having nuclear power plants is like having hens—in time they all lay eggs."

June smiled. "Harold always has food in his head. Just like his 'Confucius said.'"

"Any attempt for dominance with raw power is myopic. Julius Caesar, Napoleon and the Emperor of Japan are good examples," continued Harold.

"What are you driving at, Harold?" asked Jack.

"Back to nuclear weapons—most, if not all nations have them. And yet they have not been used in war since the end of World War II. All the battles since then have been fought with traditional weapons. We developed this bioweapon, I reluctantly agree with our President's use of this term, to prevent the further death of innocent people. If it falls into the wrong hands, like Mr. Tonga and the President said at the UN Assembly, whoever has it will try to dominate the world. If everyone has it, it would achieve the balance of power. The warring nations would not use it as they have not used nuclear weapons in all their battles."

Jerry disagreed. "It is unrealistic to just make it a gift to the world," he said. "If we do that, the probability of revealing us is like hiding a giant cruise ship in Boston Harbor. Beside, how do we do it? Let Harrison do it with his toys?"

"Jerry is right. Harold is also right," said Jack.

Jim had a question: "John, you are now involved in the super-summit science committee, appointed by the President and led by the UN. What do you expect?"

"Jim, I don't really know yet since our first meeting will not be convened until Monday next week; that is four days from now. I have yet to be informed who may be on the committee, except that Dr. Young will chair the meeting. I am sure it will involve scientists from other countries."

"Just as a precaution," warned Jack, "we will return to our posts after this meeting. Nothing will change. Of course we will not discuss the involvement of the Global Foundation. In case we are asked about this 'bioweapon,' we should express our opinions since many of our colleagues know what we do and they have read our publications. We cannot pretend we have no hypothesis or opinion, or plead ignorance. If we profess ignorance, it is a clear give away."

"I agree completely," said Jerry.

Jack and Jerry were working at the Pentagon and US Army laboratories respectively. They knew how the government worked.

"When and if we are asked, should we answer on the basis of our own studies?" asked Harold.

"Talk only about your published works," Jack replied.

"Unpublished works are only for inner circles like ours," added Jerry.

"Thanks."

"Jack, Jerry, since I am now on the Presidential/UN special committee, how much information should I give them?" asked John.

Jack considered a moment and replied: "John, you will be asked your opinion, as well as how to discover who is behind this by looking at the science. They will ask you where similar work could be done and by whom. You cannot plead ignorance. I believe there are more than just us here doing similar studies. You just tell them who they are. And don't mention us first. Mention other scientists first. Then wait."

"Thanks."

"Don't eat in the hotel restaurant with your credit cards," added Jack. "There are plenty of places to eat around here. We cannot be known to be together. We are just like ordinary scientists—giving our papers, having discussions with others, etc."

"One more thing," added John. "Jack and Jerry mentioned some time ago about ensuring of trust, among us as well as of the Global Foundation board members. We are human, and human minds may change over time. So far none of us have revealed to outsiders what we have done. In time, there is no guarantee that will not change. We have to be realistic, just like Jack and Jerry said. At the last board meeting, members also began to address this. They asked me to see if there's a possible physical or biological—those were the words used—means to ensure silence. Ms. Layug will ascertain the human angle."

There was silence.

"Yes, we need to be practical," agreed June "As we age, we change—our minds too. But I don't really know what is intended by 'physical or biological means.' "

"A chip or a tracer?" asked Ruth.

"Like a prisoner's ankle bracelet?" asked Jim.

"I thought all these gadgets were just in novels," said Ruth.

"No, not really—the CIA uses many gadgets that we have no idea exist," said Jack.

"Just a thought for now," added Harold. "There is study and a pilot experiment at the Hong Kong University. A lady scientist, I forget her name, and her team have developed what she calls a 'nanosensor.' This nanosensor can be embedded in a petri dish with cultured cells. If the cultured cells change their metabolism, the nanosensor can sense such a change. When that happens, the treatment, such as growth conditions, air supplies, etc., could be designed to counter such a change, like normal cell to cancer cell, for example. The application to humans is still far away."

"Are you seriously suggesting that a nanosensor be implanted into our heads?" asked Jim, somewhat incredulously.

"Does this nanosensor react to thoughts?" June followed Jim's thinking.

"I am just throwing this out for us to consider the realistic and pragmatic aspect of what we do—something to think about," said Harold, somewhat defensively.

"Yes," agreed Jerry, "we definitely should think seriously about it. Not that we don't trust each other. We have demonstrated that already. However, there may be a slim chance that someone—one of us or one of the board members—suddenly or subconsciously has a change of heart and reveals what we do. In addition, our associates may begin to ask questions. You know, the result would be unthinkable. We do have to keep this in mind and give it a serious consideration."

"I agree," Jim nodded.

With that said, they each took their key card and retired to their suites.

Harold and June's suites were next to each other with a connecting door.

CDC IN ATLANTA

Spring was the best time to visit Georgia. Spring flowers were all in bloom on the beautiful campus of the Center of Disease Control. If one walked the trails of the Appalachians, one would see wildflowers in full bloom as well. Peach trees were blossoming, preparing to produce the famous Georgia peaches. The buds of the sweet onions were starting to push through the soil around them. The chill of the winter had subsided, giving visitors a cool and sunny early spring.

The mood at the conference at the CDC however did not match the beauty of the enchanting south. In the conference room were nine scientists, including John and Dr. Young who chaired the meeting. Two of the other seven scientists were from the USA, two from France, one from Israel, one from China and one from Germany. All these members either knew each other personally or by reputation, therefore they were not strangers.

Dr. Young opened the meeting. "Ladies and Gentlemen, thank you for serving on this special committee. Secretary Tonga of the UN and the president of the USA asked me to convey their gratitude to you all. I don't have a special agenda. We will set the agenda as we proceed. Hopefully we will be able to solve this 'bioweapon' matter. Let me just outline what I have in mind:

1. It is pretty obvious that this terrorist agent was based on molecular biology, specifically, engineering/genetic technology.
2. Since none of us have detected any unusual materials in the cells and tissues of the victims, whatever this 'agent' was could be metabolized and self-destruct, escaping detection from our current technology.
3. The delivery system was most likely airborne.
4. Production was in a secret laboratory. Or the work was by division of labor in several laboratories, and the final product was assembled elsewhere.

Ladies and gentlemen, that is all I have so far. I would like to invite you to speak openly and give your opinions freely."

Dr. Rosenberg from Israel with the squeaky voice spoke first: "On the delivery system, for the Amazon villagers and the animals in Africa, it might be by airplane. For the soldiers and the civilians, other means would be used. Transferred by people, contact, aerosol, or food?"

"Let us concentrate first on point number one, production of the 'poison,'" said Dr. Young. "I use this word for the lack of a better one. Could it be a bioweapon? What are your thoughts?"

Prof. DuBrul from France spoke. "It could be viral. Some viruses can disappear after entering a cell; they integrate themselves into the host genome. They may escape detection."

Prof. DuBrul was highly respected for his research work. He was in his mid-sixties, stood just under six feet tall, a little overweight, and had a young-looking face. He spoke English with a charming French accent. The professor had obtained his doctorate at Yale, and had done several years' research in the Y-12 at the Oak Ridge National Laboratory in Oak Ridge, Tennessee, before returning to Paris.

"They could also be bacteria," added Dr. Reveré, the French scientist.

Dr. Revere' was in her mid-forties. With heels she stood almost six feet tall, with dark hair. Her beautiful facial features appeared to give her a Hispanic look. She spoke with an American accent because she was born and educated in the United States where her parents were diplomats. After she graduated from high school, she moved with her parents back to France. She had two doctorates—in literature from the Sorbonne and biochemistry from the Pasteur Institute. She and Dr. Rosenberg had been at the UN emergency council meeting representing their respective countries.

Dr. Wu from CDC had another idea: "We may even consider amoebas. We need to consider all the possibilities."

Dr. Wu looked like a marathon runner; he was thin, energetic, and fortyish, with a receding hair line. He had obtained his doctorate from the University of Oregon. He was a varsity runner and a reserve long-distance runner on the US Olympic team. Many assumed he was from Ethiopia because he was black. In fact, he was born in San Francisco, to a Chinese father and an African-American mother who was CEO of a major financial firm and the only black woman in that cut-throat business.

"The symptoms or rather the lack of them, is curious and very unusual," queried Dr. Young. "Remember one of the pictures taken by the poachers in the Amazon of a mother nursing her baby with a smile on her face? There was no sign of her suffering from anything. To borrow a phrase from Dr. Sabin—they seemed 'to die in good health.' Furthermore, if the agent was nucleic acid, either DNA or RNA, even if they integrated it into the genome, there may be an addition or deletion of some stretch of DNA. We have examined DNA from all the victims and animals but detected no deviation from normal DNA. With our sequence method we can detect changes as short as ten nucleotides. By the way, neither we nor the Brazilian scientists found any viral particles with our electron microscopes in the thousands of thin sections of animal tissue and that of the Amazon people"

"What if the harmful agent was less than ten nucleotides?" asked John.

"It may be possible to detect their presence if there are many. That would be a statistical problem," said Dr. Reveré.

"Protein? Peptide?" asked Doktor Kalmbach from Munich.

"Proteinases or casapsin will digest them," explained Dr. Rosenberg. "Unless they are stable, like the stable peptide that causes Mad Cow disease."

"If stable peptides were in the cells of the victims, we could detect their presence. We used the best peptide analyzers, we did not find any," said Dr. Young.

"I have page after page of zero data!" complained Dr. Wu, his frustration showing.

"Did the electron microscopy detect abnormal morphology in the cell membrane or nuclear membrane?" asked John.

"None," replied Dr. Wu. "Our Brazilian colleagues did not find any either. They also sent samples of the animals and the Amazon people to South Africa. I asked those who did the analyses what they found. Their data was the same as ours, all negative. That is, the cellular structures of all in the thin sections examined were normal."

Dr. Young's research effort proved equally empty-handed. "We have tried to determine if our thin sections of the Amazon villagers or other victims and animals have any similarity with our thousands of effects of various known poisons. But there is no match."

"We did the same. No match," said Dr. Rosenberg,

"Same in our lab. Negative," iterated Prof. DuBrul.

"Maybe they used CRISPR-Cas 9 technology?" suggested John.

"You could be right," said Dr. Young. "If so, we should be able to detect the change in the nucleotide sequence of the DNA or RNA. So far, this hasn't been the case but we still have many samples to analyze."

"We have engaged several scientists at the Weisman Institute to help. All the results are negative so far," said Dr. Rosenberg rather despondently.

Dr. Young turned to a young Chinese woman who had not spoken so far. She was by far the youngest person in the room, and looked about fifteen-years old although she was twenty-five. She was very charming. Although she was just over five feet five inches in heels, people listened when she spoke. Somehow her soft but firm diction commanded attention. She was also brilliant; at the age of ten, she had been placed in a special school for unusually talented youngsters in Beijing. She then graduated from the Beijing University at the age of fifteen, and obtained her doctorate at nineteen from the Shanghai Institute of Cell Biology which was affiliated with Fudan University. The Chinese government sponsored her to spend two years at Stanford and two more at the California Institute of Technology.

"Dr. Lee? Could you give us your opinion?" asked Dr. Young.

"I think you gentlemen are all correct," she replied. "These scientists, whoever they are, have synthesized an agent or agents to change the DNA. That is, DNA editing with CRISPR-Cas9 or similar methods. The difficulty in using this technique may not be practical. We can do that ex vivo, then transfer the modified cells into the host, i.e. victims. We could do that. But to change in vivo, especially the whole body with some trillion cells? And in a population of a hundred mammals of one species among many others? I believe that technology is beyond current CRISPR technology, but is indeed based on it. We are at least five years behind them. It could not be the work of one person, it has to be a group of top scientists putting their minds together. If I were to do that, I would select mitochondrial DNA, since mitochondria are our energy center. When I saw the victims died without suffering, a smile on the nursing mother's face, I thought about mitochondria. I am sure there might be other chromosomal genes involved. What genes, I cannot even venture to guess."

"Thank you, Dr. Lee. I believe your thinking is on the right track," said Dr. Young. "We have not been able to find any evidence or clues. It may be farfetched for me to take a guess. I will try. This agent or agents may be able to replicate and circulate in the blood stream as well as in the lymphatic fluid, while replicating themselves. It would take roughly four hours to reach all the cells. Therefore, it would take at least four hours for the victims to expire, gradually without their knowing. Let us take a break and stroll around. Our director will be here momentarily. He likes to show off our campus to our guests, especially to those of you who have not been here before."

A few minutes later, the Director of CDC, Caleb Morrison, entered the conference room with an unreadable but friendly facial expression—like all politicians.

"Ladies and gentlemen," said Director Morrison. "It is so good to have you here to resolve this deadly problem. I would like to show off our campus before lunch. My tour will take about ten minutes, if you would like to follow me."

Director Morrison led the way out of the conference room into a wide hallway, a spotless floor with pictures of well-known scientists on the walls. Among them was one of Dr. Young.

"Where you are now is the administration building. There are no laboratories here."

The hallway continued to a side entrance and exit to the outside.

"On your right is our biosafety level 4 lab building. Each laboratory has an independent ventilation and AC system. None of the windows you see can be opened. All entrances and exits have double doors. They are airtight like refrigerator doors. The atmospheric pressure inside the labs and the whole building is slightly lower than outside. As you know, I am sure you have labs like these, all personnel including janitors have to change clothing when they enter. When they exit, they are hosed down, shower, then change back to their street clothes. I'm sorry, regulations do not permit us to visit these premises.

"On your left are the general labs, from levels 1 to 3. They are all identical, and they too have independent ventilation and AC systems. The floor is not carpeted like our administration building. Janitors only clean the floors and walls, but not the benches, tables, cabinets or instruments."

"What is this square building with large windows?" asked Dr. Lee.

"We call it our country club. There are solar panels on the roof, and inside are a gym, a swimming pool, and a jogging track. It is almost as good as the recreation center and restaurant for members of the House in D.C. We will have lunch there."

There were both a cafeteria and a sit-down restaurant. The visitors were led into the sit-down restaurant, where a table was set up already. They were handed a simple menu with a choice of steak, chicken, fish, or vegetarian dishes, plus all the sides. Except for three middle-age waiters, all the waiters and waitresses were young, of college age.

"In addition to training graduate students in science, we participate in an intern program with the University of Georgia for students who major in the hospitality industry. They learn about the restaurant here. Our chefs also train them, they are not just on the floor."

"How unusual," remarked Dr. Reveré, the French scientist.

Director Morrison prepared to depart. "Ladies and gentlemen, I'm afraid I have another appointment in five minutes. Dr. Young will take over from here. And, thank you for taking the time to come. Have a good day." With that said, he gave a slight bow and left.

"What a nice man," said Doktor Kalmbach.

Dr. Young nodded. "Yes, he is a very good politician, our money man. He spends more time away from here, traveling around the country, visiting governors, House members, and so forth, to keep our budget in the black. He has a degree in hospital management. And he is able to translate hard science terminology to laypersons, to the public and, most importantly to politicians."

"Dr. Young, I see many young people around here. Why is that?" inquired Dr. Lee.

"They are graduate students or post-doctoral students. There are students from all over the country and the world working with our scientists and the medical staffs. We don't have a hospital. They do their medical training in area hospitals together with research training here. There are a small number of undergraduate students, usually seniors from colleges around here."

"Do they get paid, Dr. Young?" asked Dr. Rosenberg.

"Most of them have scholarships. We do pay some. The interns in the restaurant get paid at the same level as the professionals."

Dr. Rosenberg nodded and said, "We have similar program at Weisman Institute, minus the restaurant part."

ANOTHER AFTERNOON WITHOUT ANSWERS

After lunch, the UN-led, super-summit science committee members took a pleasant walk around the campus before heading back to the conference room.

Doktor Kalmbach had an idea. "Dr. Young, if you can find out from all or most research institutes who may be doing what we said, and any related endeavors, we may distill from this information how this agent or agents might be put together. I am sure there are many unpublished works and proprietary information in pharmaceuticals. We may glean a general picture."

"Good idea, Dr. Kalmbach," replied Dr. Young as he turned to John. "John, you are in the private sector—I am sure there is a lot of proprietary information in your firm as well as in others'. I have talked to our legal staff about getting information from the private sector. Since we are facing a very unusual situation, our legal councils have advised us that we all, including you John, should sign a non-disclosure agreement when we obtain proprietary information from the private sectors. The President told me he would give us whatever we need. He stopped short of using his power of an executive order to get propriety information for us. Of course, that is for US companies only. Maybe you can convince colleagues in your countries to do the same. That will certainly help a lot."

There was silence in the room as all the committee members mulled over the suggestion.

In the absence of any comments, Dr. Young continued. "We have reached the first base, as we use in baseball terminology here; there is still some distance to get to the home base. The production of the agent is one problem we need to resolve, the distribution of the agent is another problem."

Dr. Lee interjected, "Before we get into the discussion of distribution and carrier systems, please allow me to add a thought. Although we in China were the first to use CRISPR technology on human embryos that were abnormal and would not develop, we are far from creating fetuses. We can make genetic changes in viruses, bacteria, plants, and the cells of some mammals. Humans present a different problem and therefore require a different approach. I have been using CRISPR technology on mouse embryos. I have had a difficult time reproducing the same experiment."

John nodded. "Dr. Lee, you raise an important point. I agree that CRISPR may be involved. We have to look at other alternatives in gene technology—laughing gas comes to mind. Remember our high school chemical classes? Maybe there are other gases?"

"Yes, this may not be based on molecular biology," added Dr. Wu, thinking out loud.

Dr. Young was thinking about the germ warfare labs. Germ warfare was a curse word in the global community—hardly mentioned but every country had a center or stocks when needed, for defensive as well as for offensive purposes.

"Assuming we know the nature of this agent, we need to know how it is to be distributed or applied to the victims," said John.

John was deeply involved in the creation of this bioweapon in collaboration with his Volunteer friends and support from the Global Foundation. His background as a recipient of the Presidential Medal of Freedom and an appointee of the UN-led super-science committee meant he had to play his cards right. Instead of keeping silent, he initiated a specific focus for discussion. He did not want to initiate a diversion. In fact, it was necessary for him to keep one step ahead of the others to protect himself, his friends, and the Global Foundation.

"Physical agents, like gaseous materials, would not be difficult to apply. If so, the agent has to be able to target a particular group, like hyenas and jackals at the watering hole. How could that be done?" asked Dr. Reveré.

"Sensitivity differs in different species," said Doktor Kalmbach. "That might work. But it's not so easy to find the right dosage to target a particular individual in a population."

Prof. DuBrul expanded on Dr. Kalmbach's thought. "If it involved more than one gas, it doubles the difficulty of finding the right dosage. Also, heavy metals can be ruled out because they will not be metabolized. I think the agent has to be of biological origin."

"All known poison gas will elicit some kind of stress reaction. Yet, all these victims show no sign of stress," pondered Dr. Reveré.

"That's true," said Dr. Rosenberg. "I think we should keep this in mind. Maybe someone has invented a new poison gas."

"Even medical anesthetics induce some sort of cellular reaction," added John. "If so, we should be able to see that with electron microscopy."

The scientists paused for a moment to think through the implications of their discussion. A phone call from the associate director of CDC interrupted their thoughts. Dr. Young answered the phone and put the call in speakerphone mode.

"*Ladies and gentlemen, we regret to disturb your meeting. There is a call from the White House. Please stand by for the President of the United States.*"

After about ten seconds of a low buzzing sound from the speaker, the President's distinct voice came over the speaker: "Ladies and gentlemen, good afternoon. Mr. Tonga of the United Nations and I would like to thank you for serving on this special committee and for the cooperation of your countries. It is a very unusual global problem facing us. As I told Dr. Young and your leaders at the UN General Assembly, the United Nations and I pledge full support to find the perpetrators and the method used to make this bioweapon. We plan to put it to beneficial use, just as we have with nuclear power. Thank you again. If there is anything you need, just convey your needs to Dr. Young and Mr. Morrison. Thank you and good luck."

Even though it was less than twenty seconds, the call was a welcome break from the monotony of difficult scientific discussions.

The President's call was like a shot in the arm. Years ago, as a professor at Yale, he was voted best professor for three years in a row, a rare feat in academia. He firmly believed that encouragement was far superior to tough examination and admonition to motivate students to learn. He had carried this same perception into politics and had done well by this basic tenet. He believed a leader should have vision for a task, and let infrastructure to successfully carry it out.

"Dr. Young, Dr. Wu, you have a great president," said Dr. Lee admiringly.

"Thank you. Dr. Lee. Going back to our discussion about the poison, what is your thought about the use of gas?"

"I don't think so, but it might. If gas was one of the media, it needs to be working with some biological agent—maybe a volatile biological agent. Oh! Why didn't I think of that before? Pheromone!" exclaimed Dr. Lee. Her face suddenly lit up like a child holding a new toy. "And please, call me Kuo-Min," she said with traditional Chinese modesty since she was the youngest. All the others present were the age of her parents.

While Dr. Lee's face expressed surprise and joy, the faces around the table showed a new-found admiration. Dr. Reveré from Paris actually clapped lightly.

"Dr. Lee, that's a stroke of genius!" exclaimed Dr. Young. "It is getting late. Let us meet again tomorrow at 9 A.M. Ok? "By the way, Dr. Lee, how is Dr. Wang? I thought he might be coming too."

"Dr. Young, Dr. Wang was called back to Beijing. Actually, he sent me instead."

CASUALTIES OF PEACE

After a day-long meeting in the penthouse of the Orchid Hotel, the Vols called it a day and went to their assigned suites.

As soon as June and Harold entered their suites, they immediately opened the connecting doors. They held each other for a long time before they broke off their passionate embrace.

"It's been a long time," they said simultaneously.

"June, I cannot say you are the same as in graduate school because Mother Nature would not let us to stay young forever. But, you still turn heads. Did you notice?"

"Sort of. You are still the same, a little naughty with your wicked look—older of course. You quit smoking. I am glad."

"I'm hungry. Let's get something to eat," said Harold.

"Ok. And you still like food and never gain an ounce!" June picked up her coat.

"Let's go to the market place a couple blocks from here. I am sure we can find a good place to eat."

After a good dinner of roast duck in orange sauce, they took the elevator back to their suites. Harold stifled a yawn. "It's been a long day. I need a shower to freshen up."

"Me too," said June.

"Yours or mine?"

June squeezed Harold's arm, playfully leaning against him.

"Do we still have to move around clandestinely as Jack said?" she asked.

"Well, we just left the hotel together, ate together, and rode the elevator together, so we broke the ground rules. I think Mr. Shum arranged for us to be registered under fake names."

"So am I someone you just picked up?" asked June, laughing.

"There is no better pick-up than you. We will soon know if we have screwed up our secrecy—I am sure John will let us know. In the meantime, you can be my 'companion' I just picked up!"

Later, wrapped in the super-soft terrycloth robes, they sat on a sofa in a well- decorated living room in June's suite, looking out over the Boston harbor. June looked sober. "Harold, I will be frank with you, I am having second thoughts about all this after our first meeting. Putting animals to death is one thing, but I am not comfortable with sacrificing humans in the name of peace. I thought about it all the way home. It sticks in my mind."

"I know. All of us, except you and Ruth, have seen death on the battlefields. We were trained to kill when necessary. Jack and Jerry of course have a lot more experience than us. The thesis of 'war for peace' has been ingrained in almost every nations since World War II. May be even in human history, way back when. With 9/11, a new enemy appeared—an enemy that has no front and no face. Therefore, a frontal attack has been impossible. Some nations in the Middle East have taken advantage of the situation in the form of terrorism for revenge—religious or political."

"But still, innocent human lives have been sacrificed."

"I don't like war either. The United States was not at war for a number of years. Then suddenly, we had troops in the Ukraine about to be engaged in a battle with Russia. June, we read daily in papers about hundreds of innocent people being killed. There is a term for that, it is called collateral damage. The Global Foundation came up with our effort as a means to create peace, albeit not ideal. It has worked so far."

June got up and stood by the window, staring out at the night. "But for how long? They all have withdrawn their troops, but they are still pointing their artillery in the same direction as before. When the UN finds out who is behind what is going on, and the work done in Siberia, we will be doomed. Worse, they most likely will resume the killing. Our hard work will be in vain." She had tears in her eyes as she sat back down on the sofa.

"June, we had to take chances. With John in the thick of things, and Jack and Jerry in government service, I believe we will be OK." Harold put his arm around her and drew her closer.

"Harold, I am still—"

"So far, in the past more than six months, nobody has been killed. We have saved thousands of lives already. "

June persisted. "Harold, still—look at the collateral damage, as it was called; or, more appropriately, the casualties of peace?"

Harold sighed. "I know, it's difficult for you. We've had a long day. I am tired and I think you are too. After this meeting, I will fly back to California and you to New Orleans. Let us make the best of the rest of the time here."

"Ok. Let me change. Get your PJs and come to my place, like old times."

"I forgot to bring them..."

GETTING CLOSE TO FIRST BASE

Mornings in Atlanta started with a brief shower. Blooming flowers competed to out-charm each other. The sweet fragrance mixed with freshly cut grass gave the delegates from different nations some optimism. One by one they entered the conference room in the administration building. Although all of them had already had breakfast, the sideboard was loaded with donuts, fruit, fresh coffee, tea and other beverages.

Dr. Young and the director of CDC were already at the door to welcome the delegates.

"Ladies and gentlemen," announced Director Morrison, "you heard what our President said yesterday. He was very sincere. It was not just a political statement. For those who may not know his background, he was a professor of economics at Yale before the independent party drafted him. He is the first president without a law degree. He does not beat around the bush, as we Americans say. Let me reiterate that whatever you need, we will be happy to provide. Have a good day." With the smile of a politician, he left the conference room.

Dr. Young opened the meeting. "Ladies and gentlemen, let us begin. Please take your seats."

"Dr. Young," interrupted Dr. Lee. "I don't have the experience or knowledge of all of you here. So, if my suggestions seem naive, please forgive me." She spoke with the typical Chinese modesty of a young person.

"Dr. Lee, please go ahead," encouraged Dr. Young.

"Since we have agreed that the culprit is of biological origin, and most likely the production of which involves CRISPR technology, I suggest that we collect information on whom and which major research institutions are capable of doing work like this. Their work might give us some idea how this bioweapon agent is made. We should include the private sector as well, as we talked about that earlier."

This suggestion from young Dr. Lee was in fact what doctoral candidates must undertake before starting their research for a dissertation toward a doctorate degree. It was called literature search, since doctoral dissertations research must be original. Without a thorough search, their research might be just a repeat of past work. Every scientist in the conference room had gone through the same processes but had overlooked this point as a critical step in their current endeavor.

"Bravo!" exclaimed Dr. Reveré, clapping her hands lightly.

"We have been at this game so long we forget the fundamentals," remarked John.

Dr. Young continued the discussion: "Let us write down a few key words and phrases. When we are done, I will ask our literature research specialist to work on it. Before the day is over, we should have some data."

All the scientists turned on the iPad in front of them provided by the center, and Dr. Young set up a shared document they could all access. They each typed words and phrases. When they had finished, duplicates and redundant entries were quickly erased, and each scientist could see the sum total of their entries on the iPad in front of them.

Within thirty minutes, it was done.

Dr. Young hit a button on his phone. "Carla, would you ask the literature research specialist in the library—I'm sorry, I can't remember his name—oh yes, Hector—could you ask Hector to come in here, please. Thank you."

Five minutes later, a man in his thirties of average build and with a complexion that seemed never to see the sun came through the door.

"Thanks for coming—Hector, right?" asked Dr. Young.

"Yes, Dr. Young. What can I do for you?" replied Hector.

"We have compiled a list of key words and phrases here." Dr. Young swung his iPad so Hector could see the writing. "We would like you to search the names of the scientists and institutions in the public sector that may be doing related work. That should do it for starters. Oh, yes, I almost forgot—John, should we include the private sector?"

"Yes. I think so," replied John. "It is too important for this worldwide effort not to. We should include my firm in Chicago, AZ Pharmaceutical, also Beckman, Sinnoe in Switzerland, and Dr. Rosenberg's Weisman Institute in Israel. That should be a good start. Oh yes, and the Biological Defense Lab at the Pentagon."

"Hector, did you get that down?" asked Dr. Young.

"Yes. I probably will have it ready a little after lunch, but we may have difficulty with the private sector and labs from other nations, and of course, the Pentagon. I will try my best." Hector hit a few keys on Dr. Young's iPad to transfer the data to his own computer in his office in the library.

"Thanks, Hector." Hector nodded and left.

Dr. Young continued the meeting: "We were discussing peptides versus nucleotides. Both could be our candidates. Allow me to put forth a working hypothesis." He cleared his throat. "First, both candidates could be biodegradable, metabolized after exerting their effects. Their target or targets are the genes, DNA including both chromosomal and mitochondrial. If nucleotides, they would be able to bind to certain specific complementary nucleotide sequences. If they use CRISPR technology, they would have to know which specific sequence to bind to or inactivate, or inhibit their expressions. Then they can edit the genes. We may not be able to detect the changes because these may be just a small percentage of the total genome. The question is whether the agent is a peptide, small like that of Mad Cow Disease, or does it act like an enzyme reading a specific DNA sequence? In the latter case, it would prevent the reading by normal enzymes resulting in the synthesis of mRNA to interfere with the normal cellular activities. They don't have to deactivate the gene. They could just cover up the reading sequence for some structural genes or genes for metabolism."

"I am inclined to say it is a peptide, a degradable one, not like the Mad Cow disease," said Doktor Kalmbach decisively.

Dr. Wu was not so sure. "We do have some peptides that inhibit gene expressions during embryogenesis and their development. We also have some that activate them. These peptides are transient macromolecules which regulate development. They could be our candidates."

Dr. Wu had graduated from the University of Oregon. After his doctorate, he had spent several years in England working on blastocysts. Blastocysts were just balls of a hundred cells with two layers. The outer layer would become part of the placenta, while the inside layer, called inner cell mass, would become the embryo. He had published numerous papers. Among these scientists in the room, he was probably the most prolific publisher, both in scientific journals as well as in popular science magazines.

"In our genes," said John, "there are clusters of short sequences that regulate gene functions. There are also repeats. Their functions do not depend on how many, rather their positions within the stretch of DNA, exons and introns, for example. An effect on one or a group would modulate gene functions. Small effects may escape known analytical methods. There is a limit of a DNA sequencer. Either protein or nucleotide can do what has been done to the animals and people."

Dr. Rosenberg signaled he also had a comment to make. "Either way, these perpetrators, as your President called them, would have to get hold of the DNA of every individual in order to synthesize or edit a specific CRISPR sequence to make it effective. For the soldiers and civil servants, that is possible because their DNA, or their sequences, are most likely stored in a central computer. Good hackers can easily access them. In order to effectively affect their function, a sequence common to one species would have to be present. So far we have genes specific to multiple species—not an individual gene."

Dr. Rosenberg had been trained as a developmental biologist and had expertise in electron microscopy at a Midwest university in the United States. After a few years of post-doctoral research in Belgium, he had been recruited by the Weisman Institute to head their electron microscopy laboratory. He was a quiet man and appeared to be in deep thought all the time. He smoked a pipe for enjoyment, and occasionally a cigar.

Doktor Kalmbach added to the discussion: "The villagers in the Amazon were probably inbred for some time, so I am sure everyone shared some genes. It would not be difficult to find them. The mitochondria DNA in each individual would be identical. If mitochondria DNA is the target, it would be easier than targeting chromosomal DNA. Yesterday, Dr. Lee suggested that too."

A graduate of the University of Berlin, Doktor Kalmbach later attended Cal Tech before spending three years at the Guangzhou Institute of Cancer Research. He spoke a little Cantonese. He was on the German national basketball team playing point guard, and was a good tennis player too. He was a soft spoken gentleman and a kind person who would not harm a fly.

"Mitochondria DNA would be a good target," said Prof. Dubrul. "However, there are other genes, that when edited by whatever means may cause death as we have seen—maybe even proteins."

Young Dr. Lee had been listening without saying a word until Dr. Young turned to face her again with a questioning look.

"Mitochondria would be good targets," she said. "But I don't think just editing mitochondria DNA is sufficient to cause death in that manner. Why not RNA? If they could edit RNA, especially mRNA, we would not be able to detect changes in DNA because mRNAs are transient molecules."

"Absolutely right. Dr. Lee. We certainly need to include RNA as a candidate," agreed Dr. Young.

Just before lunch, there was a knock at the door.

Hector came in with a few copies of what he was assigned to do.

"Dr. Young. I have found these results. I also uploaded them to the iPads here in the conference room."

"Thank you, Hector. That was quick," said Dr. Young. "Director Morrison texted me that he would join us for lunch. We can look over the list after lunch. Then we can all scour the publications in detail at home. We may or may not need to meet again—conference calls may be sufficient at this point. I hate to make you all cross oceans to be here. Our President, as well as Mr. Tonga of the UN, your governments, and all of us here including myself, want to get to the bottom of this as soon as possible. We may be able to ascertain from this literature who or what group may have the capability of such advanced technology." With that said, they filed out of the conference room to the restaurant in the so-called country club.

Mr. Caleb Morrison was at the door to greet this group of experts from the international community. "I hope you have had a fruitful discussion this morning. Permit me to join you for lunch," he said. "I understand our President called. He is very sincere about this—he is not just using it as a political ladder. Many presidents in the past have used disasters as their ladders to gain more popularity—in certain cases, to get re-elected. Not this President and not at this time. Please be seated."

They were in a private dining room with windows overlooking the beautiful grounds, the scene of a typical Georgia spring.

"Thank you Mr. Morrison," said Dr. Rosenberg.

"Please call me Caleb."

"Mr. Morrison—Caleb—how many scientists are working in this center?" asked Doktor Kalmbach.

"There are 431 permanent staff with doctorates, another fifty or so visiting researchers whose durations vary anywhere from weeks to months. There are about three times that many supporting techs, not counting service personnel. Our budget is in the billions. This includes a lot of work contracted out for special projects and storage facilities as well."

"Quite an operation," said John.

"You know, John, this is a government operation. It's your tax money at work! We also do work for the UN and cooperate with other nations. This is our mandate ever since our establishment. Our current President considers health a global problem. Since his inauguration we have established satellite labs in less developed nations, some in remote regions like the Amazon and sub-Saharan Africa, to help monitor health conditions and give instructions on conducting supplemental health programs to the local task force. We also give UNESCO assistance whenever asked. As long as our budget office in D.C. says there is money, we will continue to be of service to the world." The director spoke with a proud smile on his face. The cell phone in his pocket vibrated. He reached for it. "Excuse me for a minute."

He stepped away from the table and pressed the phone to his ear. After a while, he returned to the table. "Excuse me again. Our Vice President wants me to sit in for him at the World Health Organization tomorrow in Geneva. Before I go, I have to talk to him. I think it will be on the topic you are now discussing, or on the political side of health—maybe even on the political side of science. As you know, the solution for the current event is your mission, with us on the side to help, not the politicians. But I have to go now to catch the next plane to D.C. Please, anything you need—ask one of my staff." Having said that, Mr. Morrison left the dining room.

"Ladies and gentlemen, I am sure you have that in your country too," said Dr. Young. "Let us continue our discussions. We have the information from Hector. I suggest we look them over together after lunch. Each one of us will then have a printout to take away or you can transfer them to your computer at home. I am sure we all know some of the researchers personally or from reputation. We must study their work in detail. Each of us collate a list of possible candidates, please send them to me. My staff and I will summary them into some sort of probable cohort of operation according to our discussion. Have a couple of alternatives. We can arrange for a convenient time for all of us for a conference call; then, if we need to meet again here, our Center will take care of all your travel needs. You have my email here and my phone in the office. Carla my secretary knows all of us. You can send her your requirements, 24/7."

Other than Dr. Wu, the foreign scientists were not used to "lunch meetings" even though what Dr. Young said was short. They picked up their utensils and started eating again after Dr. Young had finished speaking. There was silence as they ate the lunch, each lost in thought.

Twenty minutes later, they all headed back to the conference room.

Dr. Young restarted the session: "Allow me to make a short summation: The agent is most likely a degradable peptide after doing damage to the genes, maybe both chromosomal and mitochondrial DNA. This agent can only partially inhibit or slow down gene expression, but not totally inhibit it. The victims would not even have noticed the effects. Just like many fortunate patients who die in their sleep; all their cellular activities were shut down at once. Is that about right?"

"Yes, I think that summarizes it pretty well," said Prof. Dubrul.

"I think we should also be thinking about the CRISPR technique with peptides or RNA," added Dr. Lee.

"Dr. Lee, do you mean like Mad Cow disease but degradable? Or some RNA virus?" asked Dr. Reveré.

"The answer is yes—but not a stable one, for both peptides and RNA." Dr. Lee said.

There was no further suggestion or comments from other members of this UN-led, super-science committee in the room.

"We will need to discuss the carrier system too," said Dr. Young in closing. "But first, let us narrow down the list from Hector. Do get back to me as soon as possible. We don't want to let this drag on too long. We cannot afford to."

With that, they said good bye to each other and the beautiful Georgia spring.

BALANCE OF POWER AT HAND

It was a regularly scheduled board meeting of the core members of the Global Foundation, a month before Christmas. The whole block where the GF building was located was strung with colored lights and Christmas decorations. Even with two inches of fresh snow on the ground there was no lack of Christmas spirit. Tourists as well as locals enjoyed taking horse-drawn carriages through Central Park, down Fifth Avenue to the Empire State building. There were no better holiday decorations than New York City's anywhere. Many tourists came to NYC just to look at the decorations in shop windows.

The mood at the conference in the basement of the Global Foundation did not match the jovial mood out in the streets. It was a critical time to decide the future of the Foundation. Like the Volunteer friends, the board members had not expected such a strong reaction from the world community. With a no-nonsense American President supporting the UN-led task force, from both the financial and scientific aspects, every action taken by the Foundation had to be carefully considered, including rescue missions. There was no room for error, including the financial aspect—when the world was facing an unknown threat, the first thing governments looked at was the books, i.e. follow the money! That was the most important roadmap to catch the culprits. That was how several terrorist organizations, including ISIS, had been eliminated or reduced to a vociferous few which were no longer a threat.

After the pleasantries and handshakes they got down to business.

Mr. Erikson opened the meeting: "We are fortunate this time, there have been no delays at the airports like last year. I'm glad you all made it to the Big Apple with no problems. Professor Alvarado just texts me that she cannot join us because there is an internal political problem concerning the wellness of the Amazon. I am sure you have seen or read about the actions coming out of the latest UN

General Assembly. The UN, led by the US President, has organized a scientific super summit with the world's leading molecular biologists, including one of our own. We therefore have an inside person to funnel information to us. In a way, it is a blessing—we need that very much to chart our future course."

There was no disagreement around the conference table in the basement of the Global Foundation.

"John?" said Mr. Erikson, looking in his direction.

"Thank you. Dr. Roger and I had a good conversation before we came here. I'll let Dr. Roger update the board," he said.

Dr. Roger cleared his throat and looked somber. "I believe this is our first drawback since I joined the organization. I still believe our decision to undertake the project was the right one. John and I are the only two scientists on the board. And John in particular is in the midst of this scenario. We think that we need first to protect our scientists, John's Volunteer friends, and keep their associates out of harm's way. I am now at a retirement age of seventy-five, five years after most people. I should be the first to withdraw from the scene. Others will follow in a gradual manner, except John. He will be the last. If he retires now, it would be a clear indicator that we might be involved. John is very visible, as we know."

Ms. Layug spoke next. "Dr. Roger, you have contributed a great deal since the inception of the Foundation. One of the most notable contributions is the establishment of health centers in many outlying regions, supplementing local talent to handle emergencies and medical needs. You have trained all of them yourself."

There was heartfelt applause around the table.

"I would like to take the liberty of installing a plaque here in commemoration of your service," said Mr. Erikson.

"I will see to it," said Ms. Layug.

"John, as I recall, all the scientific associates working in Shelter 113, from the beginning to end have left their original posts. Am I right?" asked Dr. Roger.

"Yes."

"The service personnel have also left their original posts, either retired or transferred to other jobs," added DJ of Beijing.

"DJ, can they be trusted?" asked Ms. Jankovic nervously.

"Yes. They are my most trusted workers. They and their families are now very well set up for life. They actually did not know where they were. They have some idea that it was an important project, but they did not ask questions."

"Good. We don't want to take chances," said Ms. Jankovic, her relief palpable.

"No argument there," agreed DJ.

"Mr. Sonnovovitch, what about Shelter 113?" asked Mr. Shum.

"It has been sanitized, supervised personally by myself and our colleague Mr. Chuen Lo. Mr. Chuen Lo and the lab architect, Ms. Lorraine, did a great job designing it so it could be dismantled easily."

"Mr. Shum is very generous; he has given a week's stay at one of his hotels and resorts to all workers," said Mr. Kennedy. "We provided the travel expenses with Ms. Jankovic's assistance for all the travel itineraries. We worked it out so they each thought they had won a prize."

"John, how about your Tennessee friends?" asked Mr. Erikson.

"They too will retire gradually. I will suggest that to them at our next meeting. I will tell them about the discussions at the CDC, the UN, Congress and White House. I will report what I learn to you later today."

"John, I don't envy your position," commiserated Dr. Roger.

"In a way, it is good for us that I am the 'inside man.'"

After a simple lunch, they went back to the conference room.

John started his update to the board: "Allow me to summarize the three meetings I had with our President, at the UN and at CDC. Oh yes, and our Senate. Senator Ngoi is just as no-nonsense as our President. He demands to know all the proceedings of the UN-led super committee. In addition, he has organized another team to look into the matter as well. I shall try to be brief and avoid scientific jargon and detail.

"We all know about the UN meeting. At the White House, all the Cabinet members and advisors were present, plus the Nobel Laureate Dr. Young of the CDC, and myself. The President recognized me in the audience at the UN after he gave his speech and asked me to be on this special task force.

"I will now report on the most important development in the science portion. As we know, whatever we have developed will be a reality in a few years' time. We did it because we pooled our heads together with support from the Global Foundation.

"The meetings at the CDC were the most import aspect of the investigation. All the representatives were scientists—Dr. Young who chaired the meeting, one scientist from Israel, two from France, one from Germany and one from China. The scientist from China was only in her early twenties, as smart as our young Harrison and my young genius associate Alex who was only fifteen. Our President called to give us a pep talk. He called it a 'bioweapon' for selective death. We narrowed it down to what the agent would be and how it could work. Briefly, the committee actually has answers to these questions which are almost identical to what we did. Then we sought to identify which laboratories or scientists have the capability of doing this work. To do that, we compiled a list of words and phrases, and asked an expert in the library to do a search of all published scientific literature, much the same as any doctorate candidate would before they undertake their dissertation research. He produced a list, which we were given, and we each took the list home to see if it could give us hints. Next, we will meet again. The list includes publications by Jack at the Pentagon and articles from my laboratory."

"Is that good or bad?" Mr. Erikson asked.

"It could be either," said John. "Yes, I am an inside man. No, I may have to give more detail from my unpublished work. If not, I would easily give myself away. However, my work only covers a portion of the whole. That applies to Jack's too. Jack has advised me to stick to my published work. Fortunately, I cannot give out proprietary information. That is the good part, unless my work is subpoenaed by the Supreme Court, or by an Executive order from our President."

"How about Jack's part?" asked Ms. Layug,

"The Government's work is not as fast as ours in the private sector. Whatever Jack has published is at least a year behind us. So, if Jack gives them everything, it is also just partial data as well."

He added, "Jack is our senior Vol. He served in the marines for some fifty years. He can retire anytime with an honorable discharge. In time, I think all of our research will be included on the list. Some of us will retire sooner than others. We will not retire at the same time—that would raise suspicions because all of us are well known in the fields of molecular biology and molecular therapy. I will be the last to retire and stay on the board."

"I was also thinking about our Foundation," said Mr. Sonnovovitch. We certainly don't want to raise any suspicions that we are actually behind this—your President and mine called it a 'bioweapon' with a terroristic context."

"No. We definitely do not want to," agreed Mr. Erikson.

"How could the light shine on the Foundation?" asked Mr. Shum. He did not usually bother with the day to day business. But if the Foundation was suspected in this peace project, he also had much to lose because of his vast global holdings in the hospitality business.

Ms. Jankovic answered, "If there is the slightest suspicion about our possible involvement, we are doomed. All our past good deeds will be wiped off the charity charts. And our generous contributors and volunteers will leave us in droves."

"For the first time, the UN is leading a global task with backing from the USA and other technological advanced countries like China, France, and Germany. And Israel." Ms. Layug spoke slowly, the weight of her words sinking in around the table.

"To continue our charity activities, we need to remain as we are, now that we have at least accomplished our goal, although our future prospects are unknown," said Mr. Kennedy.

"We will continue our regular activities, business as usual," said Mr. Erikson with confidence, seeking to rally the group. "Keep a low profile as we have been doing. And, just a thought, we have money left over from the development of the 'bioweapon,' which is actually not a bad description. Maybe we should consider a donation to our brother and sister organizations to help with their activities. We can gradually add this to our general expenses. The US government regularly audits all charity and nonprofit organizations. There is no problem in doing that. I am actually surprised, very pleasantly surprised, that your scientific friends, John, have accomplished so much in such a short time frame."

"We could not have done so without the help from everyone around this table," replied John. "But, may I add that putting our heads together with such excellent associates was the root of the success. It will take at least five years for the molecular-biology community to do what we did in two."

"How long do you think the world will remain warless?" asked Ms. Layug.

DJ of Beijing replied, "It has been more than a year with little or no bloodshed. Will that continue another a year or longer? I don't mean to be pessimistic but I don't think world leaders have the will not to kill. They, and probably many people too, think that war is natural human behavior."

"So far, we have saved thousands of innocent lives," said Ms. Jankovic sounded optimistic. "We will save more. But in time the same or similar bioweapon will be developed. It will be like nuclear weapons; almost every country including small ones like Thailand and Serbia may have them too."

It was Dr. Roger who replied. "Ms. Jankovic, you mentioned a key word, 'nuclear.' In all these wars and battles for the last fifty years, no nuclear weapons have been used. Nations who fight know it would be the worst disaster in human history if they were used. The old term 'nuclear winter' will in fact come upon us. Every country wants a bioweapon, and every big or small pharma wants to profit by developing it. I'm sorry, but with that kind of incentive, R&D will accelerate—like we did, but with different goal. Now if everyone has a bioweapon, as with nuclear weapons, they may not use it against each other. If everyone knows the method and procedures, there will be no market."

"That is a stroke of genius. Well said, Dr. Roger," said Mr. Shum.

"Thank you."

"I think we should just let the whole world have the protocol," said John.

Mr. Erikson disagreed. "Not yet, not so soon. Let us wait until the UN special task force reaches a certain stage of progress. We then will release the secret, so to speak. I don't know how long that may be. John, any idea?"

"I don't know yet. Not until our next meeting at the CDC. I will then have some idea. In the meantime, we shall sacrifice a small number of animals not on the endangered list, or maybe even some domestic population, to keep the world leaders on their toes. Many more lives will be saved in the meantime."

"John, are you thinking what I am thinking? That we target a few animals in some very visible events, like dog shows?" asked Mr. Shum.

"That is a great idea."

"Two strokes of genius," interjected Ms. Jankovic. "There is such an event in Eastern Europe in three months' time. That may be a good prelude."

"But we have to find out whose dogs will be at the show in advance," said Dr. Roger.

"No problem," said Ms. Layug, "I have contacts in the dog show business and other social events. I will obtain a list. Most if not all the owners of these animals are well-known celebrities. And they are more than glad to be in the public eye."

"Are we in agreement with what has been proposed?" asked Mr. Erikson, looking round the table.

"I think it is a good idea—a 'balance of power,' like nuclear weaponry," said Mr. Sonnovovitch. "How long the warmongers will keep their fingers off the trigger, I don't think we can predict. And I for one did not have that in mind when we decided to carry out this bioweapon project." He thought for a second. "Maybe we should change our mantra to 'Biotech for Peace'?" he questioned, making quotation marks with his fingers.

" John, as soon as you tell us the best time for Harrison to broadcast the protocol to the world, we let the East River swallow a couple more appliances," said Mr. Erikson.

"It is still early yet. Let us occasionally sacrifice a few blue-ribbon puppies," replied John. "There is one important point brought about by our military friends, Jack and Jerry. So far we have been able to keep our project from the public because none of us has any notion of backing out and revealing what we are doing. However, we are all human, and we all make mistakes. Jack and Jerry suggested we find some way to prevent any such mistakes, albeit unintentional. We discussed the personal facet in our previous meeting on. I think Ms. Layug mentioned it also. My scientist friends are thinking about how to ensure our trust in each other. If there is a possibility for any of us to make a mistake, how can we detect it? And how do we prevent the mistake from being made?"

Ms. Layug provided the answer: "I have talked to the psychologists who helped us extract—the term used by the scientists—their associates to Siberia. By the way, Harrison here helped by hacking into the CIA computer so the associates would not be under the radar and therefore their whereabouts would not be monitored. My conclusion is that among all of us I am the only one who has nothing to lose if one of us makes a mistake. Therefore, I have no objection to being monitored."

"No, No, Ms. Layug. We are all in this together," protested Mr. Erikson. The other board members echoed in agreement.

"We did talk about the physical means for monitoring," said John. "There is a new method to sense cellular changes, possibly including thoughts. A scientist in Hong Kong developed a nanosensor to monitor physiological changes in cells and tissues for the diagnosis of diseases—what she has done is very futuristic. In other words, we may be able to plant a chip into each of us to monitor our thoughts, with a view to ensuring our trust."

Dr. Rogers was curious. "John, what was the reaction of your friends from Tennessee?"

"We have not come to a conclusion yet."

"Yes, that is something we should consider. It is too important not only for us, but also to sustain the success we have accomplished," said Mr. Sonnovovitch.

There was no further discussion and the Board adjourned.

HOMECOMING IN KNOXVILLE

It was the Homecoming in Knoxville. Under a sunny sky it was a chilly fifty-degrees Fahrenheit with a 12-mph wind, not enough to have a wind-chill factor. A steady stream of people wearing orange and white were starting out toward the Neyland Stadium. Some came as early as three hours before kick-off time for the tailgate parties. Got to have them!

As usual, hotels and motels in and around Knoxville had been booked solid on this homecoming football weekend. Some visitors had to stay as far away as Pigeon Forge, the home of Dollywood at the foot of the Great Smoky Mountains. Parties were held in hotel rooms or party rooms in all the hospitality establishments. Local residents flew their Volunteer pennants and strung up orange-and-white lights as if it was Christmas. Some residents near the campus rented out their spare rooms as B&Bs. Driveways and front lawns were used as parking lots to make a little extra money.

This Homecoming weekend was special because the Vol's arch rival Alabama was in town. Alabama was ranked #1 and the Vol ranked #6. The Vol had practiced doubly hard this season and intended to dethrone Alabama's Crimson Tide.

Since graduation, the seven Volunteer friends had been attending Homecoming games almost every year, just like all other Tennessee alumni. This year they had an additional reason to come back to Knoxville. They had received encrypted email from John telling them they should all meet before the game:

"We will take advantage of the Homecoming to have our party. There is no need to be clandestine because there will be numerous orange-and-white parties all over Knoxville. We will be staying at different hotels downtown within walking distance of each other. Just go there and check in with your families two or three nights before if you wish. Reservations have been made for all of us for four nights. Ruth, Jack, and Jim will be at the Hilton. Jerry, June,

Harold and I will be at Sofitel. June and Harold will be our party hosts. Arrange whatever your families wish to do that evening. Wear orange and white like ninety percent of people in town. The Global Foundation will pick up the tab."

From early evening before the big game, all the hotel lobbies were brimming with fans and lines at the bars were three deep. There were a few wearing Crimson Tide red. Irrespective of the color they were wearing, everyone was having a great time.

June picked up the phone in her hotel room and pressed the Room Service key.

"Hello, this is room 605. I would like to confirm my order of party trays and drinks for twenty people at 7 P.M. this evening," she said.

"Yes, Ms. June," came the reply. "Will you require a waiter?"

"No thank you. We will manage. Please clean up tomorrow because we don't know when the party will be over tonight."

"No problem, ma'am. We do this every year. Have a good time. And thank you."

After the usual handshakes and hugs, everyone settled down in the presidential suite that June and Harold shared for the next few days.

John started the meeting. "Let's get down to business. This may be our last business meeting together in one room on what our President called a 'bioweapon project.' Let me summarize what the UN-led, super-summit science committee has done so far. There were a total of three meetings hosted by the CDC in Atlanta. I will skip the details and who was present. The committee has actually concluded that the perpetrators—i.e. us— were most likely using CRISPR-Cas9 technology. The Committee's first thought we had cleaved certain chromosomal DNA and possibly mitochondria DNA. At the second meeting, a young molecular biologist by the name of Dr. Kuo-min Lee from Beijing suggested we might have targeted RNA as well. That was close to home.

"To find out who might have the capability to undertake the project, Dr. Lee suggested we do a literature search with key words, like the literature search we do before we start our research for a dissertation. No one had thought about that until Dr. Lee—who, ironically, was not supposed to be there except Dr. Wang, a technocrat at the UN, had been recalled back to China. He sent Dr. Lee in his place. In just under three hour hours, a literature search wizard at the CDC named Hector came up with a list of laboratories and scientists that may be capable of carrying out what we have done. The list included Jack's and Harold's laboratories in the US, other molecular biologists in China, Russia, Israel and one in Singapore —oh yes, a few big pharms, including mine. We took this information and the references home to study in detail.

"The following week, i.e. last week, at our last meeting at the CDC, we identified laboratories worldwide that were capable of reproducing our work. We came to the conclusion that it would take at least three to five years with the collaboration of several labs or scientists to accomplish what we have done. At that meeting, we talked about the delivery system. You guess right, it was Dr. Lee again who suggested that targeting selected individuals or animals could be achieved with pheromone-like systems like in insects. With that suggestion, in less than two hours, Hector gave us a list again. This time the list included Jerry's and Ruth's work as well as two laboratories in Israel.

"In the afternoon, we discussed whether the carrier system could be either an aerosol, or microencapsulation in micro-robots, or nano-encapsulation, or nanobots. There was one important aspect that we have developed that was not discussed. That is the self-reproduction capability of our 'bioweapon' agents after they enter the organisms, regardless of the entry point. In a nutshell, this UN-led scientific spook group was able to come into our ball park. In three to five years, our 'bioweapon' can be reproduced."

Jim was first to react. "I am not surprised. After all, there are many talented colleagues, if they came together like us, they could do it too," he said.

Harold looked worried. "What I am afraid of now is the geopolitical situation when a few countries can reproduce our 'bioweapon' or even improve upon it—sorry, that word and its factuality have got stuck on my tongue."

John continued, "The USA, China, Russia, Japan and the EU can probably develop the techniques, now that this UN-led committee has established a probable protocol, albeit on paper at this time. It will not take long to develop a complete working protocol."

"Whoever has the technique first would probably want to control the world. History reminds us of that all the time," interjected Harold with a stark warning.

"Our President, our Senate, and the UN consider our good intentions as a criminal act. There will be more special Senate committee hearings. I am sure it will generate much noise in the media. And all the senators and congressmen and women will want to get involved so they can get grants for example for their universities. At the last Global Foundation board meeting, in order to protect us, the board suggested that we should retire from our posts. Dr. Roger, one of the members, has already done so."

"I was actually thinking about it too. I have over fifty years with the military—it's time to find a fishing spot in Alaska," said Jack.

John nodded before continuing, "Oh, before I forget, I overheard something interesting, but I'm not a hundred percent sure—that China, Russia, the EU, Japan, and India have formed a special task force, or consortium, to duplicate or improve upon what we have done. Our President has indeed ordered his Cabinet, the National Academy of Sciences and the NIH to form a consortium from academia's top molecular biologists to do so. And, they are all native-born Americans, and they and their families will be protected by the Homeland. That's serious—now, back to the question of retirement."

"Actually all of us, except June, have reached retirement age, or early retirement age," said Jim.

"We should all not retire together. If we do, the government, even the White House, will be suspicious—a fast check will reveal our relationship. Almost every year we have our reunion on Homecoming Day. We frequently attend the same conference too. We are not unknowns in molecular therapy."

"I planned to quit next month and let some young person take over my lab," said Ruth.

"Good," replied John. "We have been able to keep our relationship with the Global Foundation secret. Our collaborative work on the bioweapon was kept secret also because we let our associates do the actual work underground in Siberia. So far, our associates have also kept their work to themselves as we asked them to, so I think we did select the right people. Although the scientific staff knew it was a super-secret project, they did not ask the nature. The non-scientific staff did not care to know. All of them have yet to say a word to outsiders. Ms. Paz Layug deserves great credit for putting her great personnel skills to work. Also, Harrison, our computer wizard was able to hack into the CIA to shield them from the prying eyes their whereabouts, and comings and goings in and out of the US." He paused for a minute to collect his thoughts before continuing.

"One of the discussions at our last board meeting concerned the technique we have developed. We talked about releasing the protocol to the world so everyone can have it, like nuclear weapons—for a balance of power. Since the late 1900s, one can make a nuclear bomb by reading about it on-line. There has been no killing of innocent people since we sent out the last warnings. It has been more than 12 months. But we don't know how long it will last."

"Our work is done. Our goal has been reached. What is the Global Foundation thinking?" asked Harold.

"Their immediate concerns are us. I repeat. The Foundation wants to keep us safe from all the security agencies in the world—the CIA, Homeland Security, NAS, Interpol, MI5, Israel's Mossad, the PRC Liberation Army Security, and Russia's KGB to name but a few. We talked about our retirement also. Other than me, we should retire from our activities. June is the only who has to wait a few more years to reach retirement age. Some of us have in fact and are planning on it—like Jack and Ruth. I think that is good idea and the board also agreed with what we have discussed here."

"I believe in releasing our protocol in detail to the world so no one will be the sole owner of the processes—a balance of power like nuclear power," said Harold. "We have saved a lot of innocent lives by the warring leaders heeding our warnings. We will retire, but not all together. A few months' hiatus, perhaps..."

Jim nodded. "I agree with Harold."

"Any other suggestions or comments?" asked John.

"I agree," said Jack.

"So, I will convey our suggestions to the board at our next meeting next week," concluded John.

With that said, the buddies started to relax and went ahead with their annual homecoming parties like many others in Knoxville.

Tomorrow, they would go to the game with their families along with thousands of fans in orange and white, and some in red and white.

RACE TO DUPLICATE THE BIOWEAPON

For more than a year after the warning from the Global Foundation on the potential of the bioweapon, warring nations kept their fingers off the triggers. Many lives were saved. The world seemed to be at peace and life went on as usual, at least on the surface. Underneath, storm clouds were gathering. Every country, big or small, drafted its top scientists and elite institutions in an attempt to create similar bioweapons or antidotes, to gain control, to gain dominancy.

Human nature has not changed since humans learned how to sharpen stones and make spears out of tree branches.

In the White House Situation Room—

The US President called an urgent meeting of his top staff and scientific advisors in the White House Situation Room. They included the president of the US Academy of Sciences, the Director of National Health and Human Services and Director of CDC. In addition to these scientists, the Chief of the Joint Chiefs of Staff, the National Security Council, and the FBI and CIA directors were present. Presidents of Yale, Harvard, UC-Berkeley, Directors of two top cancer research institutions, the president of Genetic Council, the US Attorney General and Surgeon General were also present. The Situation Room had never been so crowded as today; and there were more doctorates than generals in the basement of the White House.

The President signaled he wanted to start the meeting and addressed the room. "Ladies and gentlemen, thank you for coming at such short notice," he said. "I think you know the purpose of this meeting."

Everyone murmured in unison, "Yes, Mr. President…"

The President looked at every one in the room in turn. He sipped a cup of piping hot coffee. He spoke without notes. "The situation we are in with this deadly bioweapon is similar to the period after we dropped the atomic bombs Little Boy and Fat Man on Hiroshima and Nagasaki respectively. Afterward every nation tried to develop nuclear weapons. Fortunately, we have been strong enough to limit any nuclear weapon development in many nations that we consider rogue. Now, the situation is different. Biotechnology has come a long way since World War II. According to our scientific advisors, China, Russia, the EU, and possibly Japan in cooperation with India, can duplicate the same or a similar bioweapon within two to three years, may be longer. The UN-led, super-summit science committee has provided us with valuable background information. I cannot stress enough that we must develop this bioweapon and its antidote before the other nations so we can control its proliferation, like nuclear weapons, to keep the world safe. It is our top national security concern, because the security of the world is security for the USA."

"Where is Dr. Young?" The President asked his secretary, realizing the scientist was not in the room.

"Mr. President, Dr. Young has come down with the Guillain Barré Syndrome," replied the secretary. "He is in a hospital. The prognosis is that he will be out of commission for at least six months. The doctors cannot predict a complete recovery, sir."

"How unfortunate." He turned again to address the room. "Now, I want the academicians and scientists in this room immediately to form a consortium. I will not appoint anyone in particular to chair because I am not familiar with this kind of scientific research and development. I trust you can elect the appropriate person for the task. When you go back to your institutions, please identify the appropriate scientists to be members of this special consortium. And they must be all American, all native-born Americans. The Joint Chiefs, NSC, FBI, and CIA will work among themselves to provide security for these scientists and their families so they can give their undivided attention to their work on a full time basis. Again, I cannot stress the importance of this effort strong enough. All necessary funding will be from the White

House. Good day, ladies and gentlemen." With that the President left while others stood up murmuring courteous words.

At the Central Headquarters of the Communist Party in Zhongnanhai, Beijing—

"Dr. Lee, Dr. Wang, thank you for assembling this group of scientists in such a short time," said Premier K S Li. Addressing the entire group, Premier Li continued: "We have a report that the United States has assembled a group of top molecular biologists, all native-born Americans, to develop or duplicate this deadly bioweapon or similar agents. We too want to do the same. And we want to be second to none. I believe our collective effort will win the race. Spare no expense. With Dr. Lee and Dr. Wang in the UN-led, super-summit science committee, we have instant access to whatever they find, i.e. scientists capable of duplicating the protocol. And we want the world, especially the USA, to think we are not really aggressively trying to develop this bioweapon or similar agents. Like Sun Tze said, 'Keep your enemies in the dark.' And at the same time, we want them to know we are not sitting idle."

"We understand," said Dr. Wang.

"Dr. Lee, you are the youngest scientist I know. I have a special assignment for you. Westerners, including Americans and Europeans, would not suspect a young scientist of doing such serious work as we have been discussing, so you will not be on their radar. This underestimation of young people has long been their weakness in their foreign policies. Your assignment flatly and frankly, is to be a scientific spy. I want you to go frequently to the US and other nations to learn what they have done. You will go as a post-doctoral student, learn their techniques, etc." Premier Li looked the scientist in the eye and wagged his finger to stress the importance of each word, as he said, "We may be behind in nuclear and computer technology, but we will be ahead in bioweaponry."

"Yes, sir, I will do my best," said Dr. Lee. "In fact, I am going to the UN-led conference next week again in Atlanta. I will then go to Harvard's Cell Biology Laboratory to learn a new research technique. Maybe I can collect some more information then."

"Dr. Wang, I want you to chair this group," continued Premier Li. "And at the same time, remain our liaison at the UN. Would that put too much of a burden on your shoulders?" Premier Li looked concerned.

"No, sir," replied Dr. Wang. "But I do need the best communication equipment and an expert in encryption to communicate with this group when I find out what others are doing."

"You shall have it. I have other matters to attend to. Keep me informed. Thank you again. Oh, yes—there will be protective security for all the scientists involved in this task. Please tell the participants not to be alarmed." With a slight bow, Premier Li left.

In Paris—

"Thank you ladies and gentlemen. I am sure you know the purpose of this meeting," said the President of France, looking round the room full of top government staff, national security advisors, and scientists. "The United States and China are creating consortia of selective scientists, their best, to duplicate or create a new bioweapon for the purpose of dominating the world—for peace they say. Just as whoever did this, the US is the most aggressive. I have been informed that the President of the US is even involving the FBI, CIA, and other national security agencies to protect this special group of scientists, and their families—who are all native-born Americans, by the way—and the locations where they work. China is not as aggressive, as reported by our intelligence. It has also been reported that China asked its top molecular-biology laboratory in Shanghai to consider the development of such weapon. It may be just camouflage by the Chinese government, they are good at that.

"Anyway, we in the EU will not be sitting idle. It is fortunate that Professor DuBrul, Dr. Reveré and Doktor Kalmbach are all on the UN-led, super-summit science committee. We will have perhaps first-hand knowledge of the progress made by the US and China. France and the EU too would like to be able to produce such a bioweapon, if not for world peace then to prevent the continuous threat of invasion by Russian. I believe the current Russian leadership wants to create a new Soviet Union, with most of Europe under its umbrella in addition to the old USSR's hegemony."

The President of France let his words sink in before he continued. "Russia has also started to form a special molecular biology and genetic consortium for the purpose of making the bioweapon or similar, or something that can neutralize the effect. Whoever successfully develops such a weapon first will definitely have a significant influence on geopolitics. There have been no battles for more than a year now. I understand a Dr. Rosenberg from Israel is also part of the UN-led conference. We must have him on our side. Although Israel cannot accomplish the development alone, there are a few Israeli molecular biologists who can certainly lend us a hand."

"The Chancellor of Germany has agreed to contribute whatever resources are needed," added Doktor Kalmbach.

"I have talked to the Presidents of Poland, Slovenia, Italy, Spain, and a couple of large pharmaceutical firms in Scandinavian nations," said the President. "They all have pledged their monetary assistance as well as in talent. You know, Sweden is the leader in genetic engineering and the treatment of genetic diseases with that technique. We are pleased to have their cooperation. I have talked to the president of the Pasteur Institute. He will provide space and equipment for our endeavor."

"Yes, Mr. President. The Pasteur Institute has set aside space for this task." said the president of the Pasteur Institute.

On a hot line between Japan and India—

The Premier of Japan called the President of India. "Mr. President, I would like to initiate a conversation with you as soon as possible. I have learned that the USA, China, the EU, and Russia too, are all proceeding to form special scientific groups to develop similar bioweapons to the one already developed, or a solution that can neutralize it."

"Yes, Mr. Premier. I know that too."

"There will be a trade group coming with me from Tokyo to Calcutta tomorrow. Our director of the Molecular Therapy Institute and the president of the Genetic Institute will be on that plane with me."

"I will assemble relevant scientific and medical personal to meet your group."

At the Kremlin, Moscow—

In the conference room of the Politburo in Moscow there were ten people, including the head of KGB, directors of genetic engineering and medicine, the secretary of defense and other high officials. In the audience was Mr. Sonnovovitch of the Global Foundation. Mr. Sonnovovitch held the position of ex-official of defense technology and strategy.

The President of Russia convened the meeting with a short statement. "The USA, China, the European Union, Japan/India, maybe others, are planning to develop a similar bioweapon in order to control the world. Mother Russia must not be left behind. I am directing everyone here to begin a similar but stronger program. You will have support of every government department and the people of Russia. Recruit our top scientists and keep this information to yourselves. We must not let others know we are also involved. Any questions?"

"Mr. President, what is the timeline?" asked the Director of Genetic Medicine.

"As soon as possible. And one more thing—all the scientists involved must be our own. No foreign personnel or anyone born outside of Mother Russia."

THE FINAL CHAPTER

The weather in New York City was gloomy at best and depressing at worst. With an overcast sky, the temperature around eighty-five degrees Fahrenheit, and humidity at ninety percent, people walked with their eyes cast down to the sidewalk. It was not the ordinary New Yorkers' walk.

In the basement of the Global Foundation, all the core members of the board were present except Mr. Sonnovovitch.

With no more than a casual greeting, Mr. Erikson opened the meeting. "Ladies and gentlemen, we are at a crossroad. As we know, we started out with the good intention of creating a new world order of peace. In the course of a little over a year, we have saved thousands of innocent lives. Warring nations have stopped fighting each other as they have responded to our demands to lay down their arms. The heed our warnings of the consequences if they failed to do so. What we did not foresee at that time was that our agents, now called bioweapons, instigated a race to develop the same or similar weapons by all the nations that are capable of doing so, namely, China, USA, the EU, Russia, and Japan/India. The UN-led, super-summit scientific committee has done a good job identifying the scientists and institutions in the world capable of developing what we successfully accomplished. Their intention was to find the culprit, i.e. us. It was a very ingenious scientific detective work. Among their findings were John's lab, and that of his friend Jack and Harold. Since this UN-led committee includes scientists from all over the world, their findings are known to all. It appears that we have initiated a race like a nuclear race. It is a bioweapon race! Whoever develops the agent first will control the world—there will no more world peace and it is potentially the end of humanity. And we are ultimately to blame."

There was a collective gasp, followed by a long pause.

It was Mr. Shum who broke the silence. "I am not so sure we have made a mistake," he said slowly.

"How so?" asked Ms. Layug, leaning forward, hope written on her face.

"If we can turn this biological process into one that is put to good use, it would benefit the world."

"You mean, just like nuclear energy?" asked Ms. Jankovic, her eyes lighting up with interest.

"Yes, more or less…"

"If we can equate our agent to nuclear energy and give every nation the ability to harness its power, we can do the same," interjected Ms. Layug quickly with obvious excitement.

"This would only be successful if every nation engages in the development and achieves it at the same time," considered Mr. Kennedy.

Mr. Erikson held up his hand in disagreement. "No, it is not like nuclear energy. Back then there was one—and only one—leading country, and that was the United States. After World War II, only the US had the technology. The US was able to suppress the development by other nations for more than thirty years because it was strong and acted as the world policeman to prevent the misuse of nuclear power. And the world realized how catastrophic a nuclear war would be. No one dared to use it as a weapon, to start World War III. That is no longer the case."

"I don't think we can predict whether our agent can be duplicated in two or three years," said DJ of Beijing dispiritedly.

Prof. Alvarado of Brazil added her opinion: "If every nation has the technology, like nuclear energy, there will be a balance of power. No single nation will dominate, just as nuclear power today."

"That would seem to be the solution," said Ms. Layug looking distinctly relieved.

"If we release the technology to the world, maybe, just maybe, we can stop the race to duplicate what John and his Volunteer friends have accomplished," suggested Mr. Erikson.

"I think this is a good idea, and probably the only means for achieving peace, at least for a few more years," agreed Mr. Kennedy.

"Do we have a consensus to release the technology to the world?" Mr. Erikson asked as he looked at every board member in turn.

Everyone in the room agreed.

"John is in the hospital with a stroke and Dr. Roger has left Harvard for his bungalow on one of the Caribbean Islands. We need to contact John's friend to ask for the scientific details," said Mr. Erikson.

"I will contact each of them through encrypted email at once and inform them of our decision to release the details of the protocol. I am sure each of them can furnish it just as John would have done," said Mr. Kennedy.

"When we have the document containing the protocol, we will have Harrison to send it out to the world. Do we need to meet again?" asked Mr. Erikson.

"No need. Just go ahead when the Volunteer friends send you the protocol," replied DJ.

"Wait," said Prof. Alvarado. "We still have to consider the 'insurance of trust' among us and everyone involved. Just because we have accomplished what we set out to do, it does not mean our mutual trust to keep silent will continue. This may be pessimistic, but we are human, fallible just like every other human. We all age just as all human do. As time progresses, we age, we may change, albeit not purposely. Subconsciously, maybe. It is too bad John is not here to tell us if his scientist friends have come up with a solution to this issue."

"Yes. We must not forget this," said Mr. Erikson.

"We must contact one of the Tennessee scientists," added Mr. Kennedy.

"May I?" Ms. Layug said with tears in her eyes. "We cannot make decisions for the scientists or how we should proceed to ensure our trust. However, I can definitely say my personal opinion is that among us here, I am the only one who has nothing to lose if our secret is revealed. If the public finds out, Mr. Shum's hotel empire will collapse, DJ will be prosecuted, Professor Alvarado will not be able to keep the Amazon in pristine condition, Mr. Kennedy's family reputation will be tarnished, Ms. Jankovic's transportation business will be gone, and Mr. Erikson will join the rest of us. So none of you can afford to reveal our secret bioweapon for peace."

"You are right. Ms. Layug," replied Mr. Erikson, "and you are, and will always be, one of us. We all trust you and each other. But I am sure we all share the same feeling that there is never a watertight guarantee for absolute silence. Jack and Jerry know and were trained to be realistic."

"In the meantime, we must keep this in mind," said Mr. Kennedy.

Mr. Erikson nodded. "When John recovers, he—or one of the Vols—will be able to tell us how, physically or biologically, to keep us silent. If our silence is broken, it will be our responsibility to control the damage if damage control is an alternative."

One week later, an encrypted email came from Harold, saying he had the information requested and had been elected to deliver it. Instead of sending the information through the internet, he would bring it to New York in person on Monday.

On Monday, Harold took a cab from Kennedy Airport to the Global Foundation in Manhattan. Ordinarily there were no city surveillance cameras on this block, only the one operated by the Global Foundation. Harold rang the bell and was let in.

"Thank you for coming, Dr. Harold." Ms. Layug shook his hand.

"Glad to. We decided that personal delivery would be the safest means to transport this important document." He then added, "Oh, yes, my friends and I suggest that we do not release the information about the program for 3-D production. We let them just have the wet tech, i.e. step-by-step procedures used in a laboratory."

"Dr. Harold, my thanks." Mr. Erikson extended his hand and guided Harold to his office. "I will call Harrison to send this out. Before I do, the board has discussed the subject of ensuring trust that was brought up by Dr. Jack and Dr. Jerry. What have you decided?"

"Yes, we have discussed that in detail. Briefly, we know there is a new technique to monitor cellular physiological changes. It uses a nanosensor embedded in a strategic location in the body to diagnose diseases. It monitors small physiological changes that cannot be detected using conventional techniques—it uses a chip, like a tracer in pet dogs. All of us will be able to monitor changes in any of us. No one person will be in charge. We all will deal with it as a group. How we will do this, I do not know, but that may be the pro side. On the con side, we need a specialist to do the implantation of the chips. That will increase any suspicion of wrongdoing, so to speak. The specialist may ask why we would want to implant a chip into the body of a number of scientists and well-known personnel like yourself and other board members."

"I understand. The board has also discussed this matter. It is a reality we must face. So far we have all trusted each other. If our secret gets out, not only we but all the associates and workers involved will be affected too."

"Our task is not finished, not yet."

"I agree. I will call Harrison." Mr. Erikson picked up the phone.

A few minutes later, dressed in faded jeans and a T-shirt with the words "Our world, no war" printed on it, Harrison entered the office.

"Harrison, another important job." Mr. Erikson handed Harrison the laboratory protocol to produce the agent, known as the bioweapon, to be made available to everyone from the United Nations to South African safari lodges.

"Harrison," said Mr. Erikson, "we have decided to let the world know how we created what we did, but we are not releasing the program for 3-D production. This way there will be a balance of power, and there will no race to achieve what we have done. No one will dominate the world, just as no one can dominate it with nuclear power. No gene warfare."

"No problem. Just make sure I will have a new refrigerator and a new dishwasher again!" Harrison said with a smile on his face.

The next day, Harrison sent out a message to the world:

"To all nations: We appreciate that you have ceased fighting and many thousands of innocent lives have been saved. We regret that we needed to sacrifice animals and humans to convey our message.

There is no need for you to race to develop the same agent or agents that can neutralize what you call bioweapon. We have decided to reveal the details of the protocol so every nation with a modern molecular-biology laboratory can duplicate the procedures and reproduce the same agent and delivery system that we developed."

With that statement were seventeen pages of detailed laboratory protocol. They were sent out from Harrison's pad in Brooklyn. Minutes later, a panel truck with a *Trucking with Care* sign on the side drove up to the entrance of one of the houses where Harrison lived. A new refrigerator and a new dishwasher were unloaded and unwrapped. Two men in overall uniforms went up to Harrison's pad, came down with the old refrigerator and dishwasher, and loaded them into the truck. They then carried the new units up. As soon as that was done, the truck went directly to the landfill in the East River.

No neighbors bothered to even look at the truck—it was just a routine delivery in a big city.

At the landfill, the lone person on duty did not bother to ask questions, he just waved the truck to the ramp. Later, he would drive his bulldozer, pushing all the discarded appliances and rusty machinery into the greyish water of the East River to be part of land reclamation. His job was repeated many times a day.

Harrison and his friend started to set up their new toys paid for by the Global Foundation.

The merging of ancient percept with the modern ritualistic technology saved thousands of lives.

The curtain of a noble act was drawn closed.

EPILOGUE

During the next several years there were no wars, therefore thousands of innocent people were spared from death. However there were still small tribal conflicts in Africa and deep in the Amazon because poachers on both continents periodically reported seeing the corpses of people that had been killed with conventional weapons.

The Global Foundation continued its charity rescue work but scaled back, no longer sending staff and volunteers to faraway places. Gradually, the organization was dissolved and the vast amounts of accumulated funds were distributed to organizations like the Red Cross, the Salvation Army and one particular charity in Vancouver headed by Arthur Lee, MD, who founded a foundation for the blind. Full-time employees like Mr. Triple E, Mr. Kennedy, and Ms. Paz Layug also took retirement. Other board members also either retired or went back to their respective businesses.

The role played by the Global Foundation in the creation of a bioweapon for peace was buried in the landfill in the East River, New York City. The nameplate of the Global Foundation in the modest brown stone in Manhattan was replaced by the sign of a legal institution.

Jack and Jerry were honorably discharged from their military posts. Jack went north to Alaska to find his fishing hut. In the summer, he flew a hydroplane for tourists to other fishing spots. In the winter, he was a snow bird who returned to North Carolina to spend time writing at the place that had been his family's home for three generations.

Jerry and Carol went back to East Tennessee to live near their sons and daughters. Jerry took up his father's profession of cattle ranching; he had just a few animals so it was more like a hobby than a job—he was a gentleman rancher and farmer.

Jim resigned from the research institution where he worked for some thirty years, and found a teaching job at a small college for several years before retirement.

In the meantime, John had recovered from his stroke. Since he was incapable of working again in the laboratory, he too retired to San Diego, near the beach.

Ruth almost died from a rare form of cancer. However, just as suddenly, she recovered and retired back to her southern city and married her childhood friend after he lost his wife.

One day Harold picked up a phone and called June. "June, how are you in the humid and hot city of New Orleans?"

"Well, I am sweaty and hot and trying to fight off the mosquitoes on my riding lawn mower! "

"Why don't you get a kid from the neighborhood to do it?"

"Laugh all you want, I like to feel the breeze wearing my floppy hat."

"The reason I am calling is that I too have submitted my retirement request. A long time ago, I collaborated with a marine biologist in Costa Rica and went down there several times. My wife Rose was alive in those days, and once she came down with me. We took a tour and passed by a small, out-of-the-way village on a mountain top, where the air was cool even though it was ninety degrees in the valley and on the coasts. We saw a for-sale sign. After the tour, we went back and bought..."

Without listening to what Harold would have said, without hesitation, June exclaimed, "I am flying out on the next flight. Don't you dare leave for Costa Rica without ME!"

Q.E.D.

THE AUTHOR

Harold H. Lee was a professor of biology with a specialty in embryology at the University of Toledo, Toledo, Ohio, USA. In addition to his teaching duties, his laboratory research led to his earning several US and Canadian patents in biotechnology, including instrumentation and bioremediation with biodegradable natural materials. After his retirement, he began to contribute articles to a variety of health-related magazines on the use of Tai-Chi, the martial art, to improve health. *Casualties of Peace* is his first novel. A sequel entitled *"Echo of Peace"* is in the works. He resides in Mission Viejo, California, USA.

Made in the USA
Las Vegas, NV
27 January 2022